MW00943199

For
Pam Matthews
and
family
for their reading
pleasure
(I hope)
[illegible signature]

Journey to Little Rock

by Fred Sanderlin

authorHOUSE™
1663 Liberty Drive, Suite 200
Bloomington, Indiana 47403
(800) 839-8640
www.AuthorHouse.com

This book is a work of fiction. People, places, events, and situations are the product of the author's imagination. Any resemblance to actual persons, living or dead, or historical events, is purely coincidental.

First published by AuthorHouse 11/16/05

ISBN: 1-4208-7987-1 (sc)

Printed in the United States of America
Bloomington, Indiana

This book is printed on acid-free paper.

Cover design and chapter illustrations by:
Peg Archambault

Remembering Otha Lee and

Guy Arnold

Warren and Fellie

With all my heart

TO JOAN

With gratitude

in helping take this story out of the desk

drawer

Sandy & Marilyn, Bud & Doris, Hazel Lee &

Paul, Marilyn & Joe, Neat, Billy Fay & Wanda,

Charlotte, Sherri,

THE book club, and Tom & Pat

TABLE OF CONTENTS

PROLOGUE

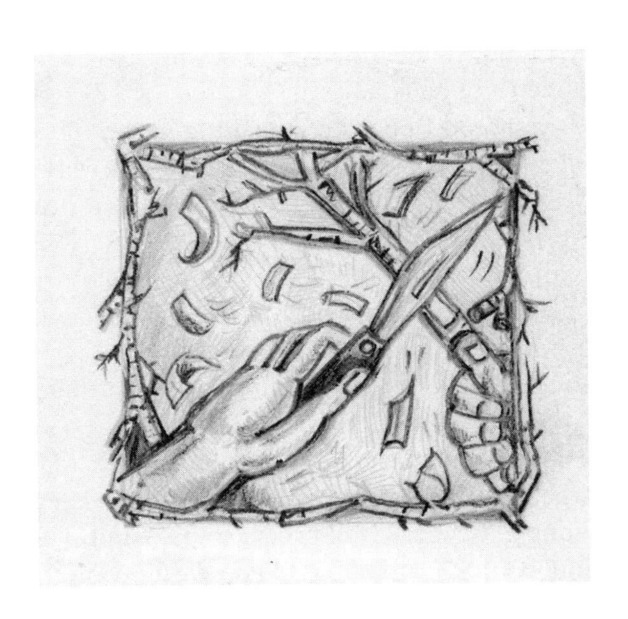

THE SENATOR

Once, while the old coot and I were fishing off an Arkansas river bank, he said he wanted me to give his eulogy if he died.

" 'If?' What do you mean 'if' you die?" I protested.

"I'm pretty busy. Might not have time for it."

"Oh, you'll have time for it. Even you—believe me."

"Why should I believe an old boy from Mountain View, up in the Ozarks, when he betrayed his Baptist roots to wear a Bishop's miter and lead the largest diocese in the wonderful state of Arkansas?"

I came right back at him.

"Why should I consider speaking at the funeral of the longest office holding state senator in Arkansas history, when he twice turned us down in a draft for the governorship."

"Yeah, I did, didn't I?"

"Twice! Sure winner both times."

He snickered at me.

"You still have your robes in a knot over that, don't you?"

He grunted and set the hook on a fish that had submerged his bobber. He lifted the bamboo cane pole and swung a meager-sized bream to his hand.

"You wouldn't run because you didn't want to have to pull off those overalls you wore to legislative sessions all your life and have to fit into a suit just like every other state executive."

"I was holding out for the presidency."

He unhooked the struggling fish and tossed it in the wire basket dangling from the bank of the river.

"What about that eulogy? Will you do it?"

"If I'm to extol your virtues and achievements I'll need to know how a sharecropping third grade dropout rose to such prestigious heights."

He stabbed a fresh cricket on his hook and dropped his line back to the exact spot he had dragged out the other fish.

"Well, I've a notion it all began with a rooster—"

He put the pole aside, took up a branch from the ground, opened up his pocket knife and commenced to whittling that stick and telling a story I was surprised I'd never heard before—it might have been one of his yarns he was famous for stretching. But later that week, for proof, I went to the archives and read the 1910 Arkansas Gazette accounts of the crime. Sure enough, there was this photograph of a little boy ten years old, WC's big ears a dead give away, who was responsible for the capture and prosecution of two desperadoes.

So let me get my jack knife out, find me a good sized branch and tell you his story. It did begin with the sorriest of chickens.

CHAPTER ONE

THE ROOSTER

That old rooster, Gabriel, was on the roof again above his window. Nothing scared the old bird and he dared go anywhere. The boy woke to the devilish clicking of its toe nails on the shingles and the dull *thud-thud* of its pecking.

"Good Lord," he mumbled into the corner of his pillow. "Get off the roof, you flaggle feathered, ol' naked necked pound of ornery."

The rooster sassed back, crowing defiantly at the sky, stretching its neck and disheveling its few battle battered feathers. The boy grumbled and raised his face from the feathered pillow and flopped to his back. "Ain't no use quarreling with you except with a stick."

Side pork fried, sizzling and spattering, in the next room of the cramped house. He smelled it and heard his mother humming a gospel tune, while impatiently tapping the iron skillet with her turning fork. Though she loved music, music of the church the most, her rhythm clanged, "For crying out loud, won't you hurry. I have a million things to do today."

The boy knew it was time to get up, but he did not want to do it, particularly at the heartless summoning of that ruffian rooster. He would just as soon wring its miserable neck and be done with it.

Instead of entertaining such a worthless idea, he sat up and swung his legs over the side of the bed, rustling the corn husk mattress. He yawned, opening a gaping hole into his narrow face; the sun-toughened skin pulled tightly against his broad, beakish nose and across his high cheeks. For someone only ten years old, he had an older face, sluggish and sad, made heavy looking by a stack of black hair, which no amount of water or tonic would ever conquer and lay down. His thick eyebrows composed gravity over blue eyes armed with the deepest emotional restraint. His ears stood prominently from his head, like question marks, and were the only remaining signs of his boyhood—the last untouched aspect of innocence not worn away by grinding labor. A mustache would have completed a picture of a tired man.

Old Dedge's hand-me-down long johns hung on his skinny frame like a rag draped on a switch. He pulled at where the top had slid off one shoulder. "A field doll, that's what I am. A dad-blamed scarecrow." He yawned again, into his hands, ending it with a rolling growl, before falling back onto the bed and mashing into the mattress.

The boy was still tired, the night's rest not equaling the mending his slight body needed after the hours, the days, the weeks of work that had drained him with the season's final cultivation, putting the fields by. But they all were finished for now and he had that accomplishment to hold to. Not that he gave the idea of completing anything much thought—there was always more to do. Like his daddy said, "There'll always be another stone in your shoe that you have to pull off and shake out." But for the time being it felt good that the fields were done until harvest time, though his body ached. He rubbed at the soreness in his thighs. But complaining was not in him and so weariness was tucked under the coming of another day.

"Besides," he thought, "if things are ever to change, they're not likely to do it if left to themselves. You have to get up."

He pushed off the mattress and slid the short distance to the floor, landing on the bib overalls that had crumpled there as he kicked out of them the night before, too tired to bend over. He felt for them, turning them over, fumbling in the dark for the bib and straps. He hesitated stepping into them.

"Sometimes, it's the hardest thing to do to put your pants on."

A rectangular halo of yellowish light from the main room feebly outlined the burlap sacking that curtained off his sleeping nook. The boy stepped his right foot into the leg of the pants and then slowly crept his toes toward the light at the bottom of the drape. When his toes glowed and he could make out the ridge of his instep he stopped. It was stupid he knew, but he tried to see what was going on in the other room—who was there and what the mood was. He wanted to know and not be known—especially by old Dedge. He pointed them left and then right, wiggled them for better focus, but there was nothing to be seen by toes.

"What's the matter with me this morning?"

He pulled his clothes on in earnest, stuffing the abundance of inherited long underwear into his overalls, bouncing and shaking, until the material bunched at his knees fell to his bony ankles. He slung the strap over his shoulder, fastened it to the brass button, and then pulled back the edge of the curtain to peek into the main room.

His mother stood at the sink at the far end of the room, the eternal apron already wrapped around. Her hair, braided and woven into a bun at the back, gave her neck the appearance of yielding, or at least of gentleness that bordered on docility. She was a small woman, dainty to be more accurate, but for her size and slenderness she had unusually long arms. She once told the boy they were her wings, except God had left off the feathers. She resembled a bird, given her narrow face, sharp nose, small dark eyes and quick manner in which she moved.

She stood with one hand on her hip filling the coffee pot with water from a dented lard bucket. Old Dedge was not to be seen. The spitting can was gone, so the old man was off outside with his first plug of tobacco.

"Good," the boy's spirit rose. It was not often he and his mother were left alone. He would make the most of this rarest of times.

"Lord!" she cried, "Oh, my Lord," and dropped the coffee pot into the sink and hurried to the stove, where she fanned at the smoke billowing from the skillet.

"What a mess." She grabbed a wad of dishcloth and picked up the smoldering cast iron pan of charring side pork and placed it on the warming shelf of the stove, away from the heat. She found her turning fork and stabbed several pieces of the meat, lifting them dripping out of the grease.

"Oh, not so bad. Just around the edges a little. Not so bad."

Her shoulders sagged.

"Who am I kidding? He'll hate it."

The boy watched his mother reach for a plate and drop the pieces of meat onto it. She turned and set it on the table and called for him. It was her no nonsense voice.

"WC. Time to get up."

From his room, just off the center of this little world, it was comical to watch her—thinking she was alone. She tore off a piece of meat, tasted it and then nodded reluctant approval She shook her head, picked up the plate and carried it to the slop bucket under the sink where she almost dumped the meat, thought better of it and pulled the plate back. She argued with herself, muttering explosively as she weighed one thought against the other thought. Save it? Throw it away?

Her pantomime fascinated him; she was completely oblivious to any other presence. What fun to see her so natural, unguarded in every expression and gesture. The performance brightened him, leaving drowsiness and fatigued muscles somewhere below sheer delight.

He heard her say, "Shoot, I'll eat it myself," and something else about not wasting food like other fools. She carried the plate back to the table, set it down and walked back the few steps to get the coffee pot and set it on the stove. Then everything about her seemed to slump, as she stood there waiting for it to boil.

Just that quickly, he felt sorry for her standing before that hot stove, blue smoke hanging in the air, both hands on her hips seeming to prop herself up. It was the first thing in the morning and she seemed used up already. Maybe he could make her feel better.

He pushed the curtain aside, crept around the table and tapped her on the back, startling her. She squealed and turned on him, both hands held protectively at her chest.

"My Lord! WC, don't you do that." She grabbed his arm and shook him. "Don't ever do that."

"Hey! Let go of me. I didn't do nothing but tap you on the back."

He jerked away to the corner of the table to pout. His action and look were so instinctive they took his mother by surprise, being so contrary to the adult ways he liked to put on. It was an image she had not seen in years—so child like, just the way a boy should look when his feelings have been hurt: arms crossed against his chest, bottom lip stuck out like a blistered sausage and his entire upper body hunched into one screaming muscle.

Oh, it amused her. It tickled her to see her son look like a boy again. She raised her hand to her mouth and laughed.

That shocked him. Laughing? Right out loud. When was the last time he had heard that in this house? He could not remember.

"Hey?" He wondered. "Was she laughing at him?"

"What's so funny?" he demanded to know.

"Something just struck me."

"But you burned the pork. He's going to be mad."

"I know it. And you scared the living daylights out of me. But I see you standing there all knotted up, about to throw a fit, and it does my heart good. You look so young right now and that makes me happy. I can't explain or know the reason why, but I like it. Oh, I like it."

"I know why."

"Then you better tell me."

"It's just the two of us for once. That's why. We don't hardly ever have this chance together."

" 'Just the two of us,' " she repeated smiling. "You may be right. How did you get so smart, on top of being handsome?"

She thought a moment, pressing a finger to her lips. Another smile broke out and she pointed at him.

"Now what?"

"You want to dance?" She spread her arms before him and swayed to some imagined tune. "C'mon, be my little beau."

"Dance?" He pulled back as if she were diseased. "I'm not looney."

"And you think I am? Before he comes back, let's dance."

"No. I should hunt up eggs for breakfast."

"And I should slice and cook up another batch of meat."

She took his hands and swung them back and forth as she padded lightly in her bare feet.

"La, ta, ta, ta-ta-ta, ta, ta. C'mon, move your feet."

WC stumbled reluctantly, moving only when her motion pulled him off balance. Finally, she let him go and danced alone, gliding with her eyes closed. He watched her circle the table, but when she held the dingy apron elegantly away from her homely work dress, he was too embarrassed to watch and wanted to put a stop to it.

"I can twirl you, Ma"

"I think I'd like that," she purred and curtseyed to him, misunderstanding his intentions.

He closed in, locked his arms around her hips and lifted her off the floor.

"My Lord, what are you doing? Put me down, before you break your back." She began laughing. "I said, turn me loose, WC. You'll hurt yourself."

She was more weight than he had judged. He staggered into the wall, ricocheted away and glanced off the table. A jar of fresh cut blooms wobbled and a ring of water squeezed against its bottom.

"Watch out, you'll spill my flowers," she continued laughing and held his shoulders.

He fought for balance between the table and wall, spinning, his breath chugging. With a mighty act of will, he stopped his momentum, bent his knees slightly, and straightening, he tossed her a little higher in his arms giving him better control. Then the dance really began.

He twirled her faster and faster. They spun away from the table, passed by the sleeping nook, crossed her bedroom door at the end of the house and returned back along the sink toward the stove.

Just past the bedroom it was no longer a laughing matter to her and she began insisting he stop.

"I want you to put me down. I'm getting dizzy and likely to get sick if you don't quit."

He finally set her down beneath the kerosene lamp hanging from the bare rafter above. She stood glowing, out of breath, collecting herself. She wiped hair that had been whipped into her eyes back onto the crown of her head and wondered how she had let herself go like that. Acting like some city girl—like someone who had not burned a skillet full of side pork, who did not have to sweep and scrub the floors, who did not have a tub of washing to look forward to, who did not have to pick pickles and beans before considering setting the table with lunch and supper. Who did she think she was anyway?

Her thinking hung there, grim and insisting; the overhead light molding great thumb prints of hollow shadows beneath the ridges of her eyes and cheeks. She bowed her neck.

"Ma? Ma?" WC touched her hand. "Did I hurt you?"

She caught his hand and pressed it to her stomach, then raised her eyes and looked into his face.

"Oh, my. What have I done to you?" she whispered to herself. "You're just a boy; nowhere near a man."

He pulled his hand away. "What do you mean? I do everything around here." He crossed away from her, to the other side of the table.

She followed close behind. "That wasn't meant for you, Son. I was talking to myself. Besides being a boy is not a crime or something to be ashamed of."

"I'm not just a boy," and again he retreated a step away.

She dropped into the chair, not wanting to crowd him more.

"I know you're not. You grew up too fast after your daddy died. I let you do it; we wouldn't have lived without it."

And she wanted to take him in her arms. But she dared not, afraid he would pull away from such intimacy altogether—so conscious of his strength, born of labor and meanness.

"If I could," her words choked and broke off. "Lord, if I could, I'd hold you back—to save the boy in you. Almost all of it's been stolen."

She pointed a finger and then shook it at him smiling.

"But thank the Lord, I'm going to hold onto to whatever's left." He let her take one hand. "Hold on with everything I've got."

She scooted forward in the chair and slowly reached out cupping one of his ears in her other hand.

"Your ears are just like your daddy's: big enough to hear a spider weave."

An apron strap had fallen off her shoulder. He slipped it back in place. "I knew I could twirl you."

She stood up. "And I'm proud as daylight you could do it. But you sure are full of yourself this morning. What's gotten into you?"

"Nothing has gotten into me. What's gotten into you, ol' miss dance all over the house?"

She chuckled and curtseyed to him. "You may in fact be getting bigger, young man, but don't let it fool you into thinking you can sass your ma."

He darkened and frowned at her. Even in jest he did not like being corrected. "Don't treat me like a baby."

"And don't be in such a hurry. There's plenty of time to be a man." She tousled his hair.

"Quit it. I hate that." He ducked away from her hand and covered his arms over his head.

"Wait a minute," she said and aimed a finger at him. "You stand right there and don't move." She backed toward the bedroom, grinning and holding him in place with her finger.

He sighed hugely and shifted his weight from one foot to the other.

"Uh, uh," she warned. "I said, 'don't move,' " and she stomped her foot playfully, holding the boy faster than any anger could ever manage.

She turned into the bedroom and only a moment later came out presenting a large toothed comb.

"This ought to do it," she announced, and thwacked it against her hand several times before stabbing it into some imaginary victim. She dropped it into an empty jar and filled it with water and crossed back to the table where she sat in front of WC.

"Let's wet this hair down and see if we get some of the wildness out of it. Who knows, you might be easy to look at. Pull yourself a chair up." She gestured to a place in front of her.

He hesitated and looked at the floor, shaking his head back and forth. "Ma, I don't want to be fussed with. I got to collect eggs."

"And I have meat to fry, a house to clean, clothes to wash, and a million other things to do before I die. But they're excuses right now—things keeping us from holding on to each other. For some reason you're in a mood—I'm for sure in a mood—and I'm taking advantage of it."

Her back stiffened and her words accelerated with heat.

"You hear me? By the good Lord, I'm your ma, and I'm telling you to pick up that chair, put it in front of me, sit down and let me comb your hair for what little time we got."

Her eyes wetted, but she refused to blink tears.

Neither one of them moved or said a word. He could not hold her eyes any longer, but looked away, looked at the water sopping under the jar of flowers. He lifted them and wiped the water with the sleeve of his long johns.

"I plowed all the fields this spring."

"That you did."

"And it was me worked the harrow and planted the seed?"

"All by yourself behind those gassy mules."

He squinted at her briefly, before picking at a wart at the base of his thumb.

"I believe if I can do all that, I can lift up this little ol' chair." He moved the chair and sat in front of her.

"Your eyes shine," he told her softly. "Did you know I can see myself in them?"

"I hope so, Son. I truly hope so."

He offered his head as to an executioner.

She dunked the comb several times into the water and began tugging it through the thick tangle of his hair. Without their voices the room seemed to resonate with sounds of the comb catching in the snarls of his hair and the pulsing of the coffee pot as the heat rocked it on its uneven bottom. Otherwise there was stillness. No muscle tension. Even the surviving one armed rocker pushed back into the corner seemed to relax. There was only "Now", with the rhythm of the drag of the comb, the release of the knot, the wetting, the wiping of the drips running down his forehead. There was no future or plan, even if one was needed. No past or pain, though enough had been suffered. This time, this element of grooming was immediate and merciful. All was close.

The smoky remains of the blackened pork rolled sluggish and blue in the early sunlight angling in the kitchen window. The murky Swiss curtains seemed to be dissolving, and one dared not wash them again.

An expansive cobweb hung taut and delicate high in a ceiling corner. It would not be tolerated, but she would sweep away the spider's persistent work following breakfast. Tired, calcifying jars of tomatoes, hominy, and green beans huddled shoulder to shoulder on the raw pantry shelves.

The luxurious stillness. The entire scene, poor as it was, brought such possibility to them—its redemptive intimacy felt through the pull of the comb and the smoothing softness of her following hand.

And then the screen door whined and screeched open.

The mother wrenched and rubbed her eyes dry with the knotty calluses on the flat of her hand.

WC stood and scrapped the chair to the end of the table. He hung on to the chair back and ducked his head.

"Ya burned the pork, didn't ya, Della?" The stinging, nasal voice came from the door just before it slammed shut.

"I did indeed, Dedge."

You would expect the man standing at the door to have such a waspish effect, for he seemed to have been squeezed through an inadequate opening. Dedge was long and sinewy, though not much taller than Della. His face was nipped and edgy, bristled by graying whisker stubble. It was the exaggerated Adam's apple on his elongated neck that fascinated WC. He often stared while it bobbed up and down, infuriating the man.

Dedge's body sloped to his right side, weighted on the cane he leaned on. He could stand and walk without it, for he often swung it, or poked or prodded anything weaker. He used it on the animals, this woman he had married three years earlier, and her son. Now he raised it and pointed it at WC's head.

"Ya look plastered. What ya got, a wet kitty on yer head?" He snickered, his shoulders hunching and Adam's apple throbbing.

"Please don't start first thing this morning," Della urged and carried the jar and comb to the sink. WC followed, stood behind his mother, and yanked a dish towel off the wall rack and rubbed it over his head.

Dedge looped a stream of syrupy tobacco spit dead center into a can he held in his left hand. WC looked out from under the towel and scolded, "Ma doesn't want you chewing and spitting in the house."

"Ya little chigger, don't tell me what to do."

Dedge limped into the room. His cane struck the floor and his left leg dragged. *Thud, scuff, thud, scuff.*

"I don't see any eggs. Ain't ya done yer chores yet?"

"No, and I don't need to be reminded." He spoke directly to the lump protruding from the open collar in the old man's shirt.

Dedge shook a warning finger at WC. "Ya better watch yer mouth."

Then he turned to the mother and whined, "I'm begging ya, Della. Make this prissy little thing behave himself. I've listened to all the crowing I intend to hear this morning."

Della met him at the table. "He's wrong to talk to you that way, but he can be provoked as much as anyone."

"Don't excuse him, when he's challenging me."

"I'm not. I'm telling you what part you play."

"Woman, there's nothing I want to hear from ya. So there's nothing to tell me. Just straighten out yer little rooster, before I put a bend in his neck."

She turned back to her son. "Quit saying whatever hateful thing comes into your head. No matter who sets the example, it's not right. And, I will speak for myself when I have something to say. You hear?"

He looked away from her.

In the following silence, she took the towel from him, folded it in half and hung it back on the rack.

"Go on now, and do your chores."

"Yeah, ya go do them chores, Squirt. Bring in some eggs first. I'm hungry."

"It's not right for a grown man to torment a boy that way. I want you to stop."

"And I want ya to learn to cook decent food and not burn everything." He grabbed a handful of the meat and flung it against the wall. "Slop for the hogs."

WC bolted for the table, slid in a chair and began gathering up all the darkened meat that had rolled beneath it.

Della tried to pull him up. "Leave it and go outside." She knew the two had to be separated—things were unraveling.

Dedge waggled the cane at him. "Yeah, boy, don't make me tell ya again to get the eggs."

WC shoved all but one slice into a front pocket. He rubbed that one on his pants before chewing off a bite.

"I don't know, old Dedge, taste good to me."

Dedge smiled. "My, my, ain't we brave this morning. Just like a rooster, more nerve packed into yer head than brains." He spit into the can and stretched to set it on a shelf over the stove.

Della turned WC and began pushing him toward the door.

"Get out and do your chores. Do as I tell you! Right now!"

Dedge watched them over his shoulder as he moved to dominate the far end of the table.

"Ya better slap his jaws, unless yer leaving it up to me. I won't have some tail-dragging boy playing the rooster in my house."

WC slung away from Della.

"It's not your house!"

He was volcanic with rage—both hands fisted, body tremoring and eyes bulging.

"This is daddy's house! He cut every stick and shingle. You don't belong here, old man! You never did!"

Della grabbed him around the waist and tried to carry him out the door, legs and arms flailing. She moved him only two steps before he twisted from her grasp and erupted free.

"You're a thief! You and your brother! That's the only reason you're here."

He commanded the opposite end of the table, panting fiercely, glaring at the knob on the old man's neck.

Della held the door open. "WC, get out of the house and get the eggs."

Dedge pounded his cane on the floor. "I'll run him off the place!"

"You'll do no such thing, Custer Dedge!"

He dragged toward WC.

"If it takes a beating everyday he'll learn to keep a civil tongue or stay out of my way."

Della shouted and came between them.

"No! You're not to hit him, I've told you!"

"Move out of the way, Ma."

"Stay out, woman." Dedge swung his free arm through the air. He pointed it imperiously at Della. "And don't raise yer voice to me. I won't have him defying me and ya getting in my way."

He was quivering. Tobacco juice leaked and stained each corner of his mouth.

WC pulled at his mother.

"Don't stand there. Get back."

Dedge switched the cane to his left hand and swiped Della aside. She fell headlong onto the stove, reaching out to stop herself.

She yelped, recoiling off the hot surface, and then gave a whimpering cry. An astonishing sensation erupted throughout both her hands. It was not pain at first; it was awe and sickness, a wave that went to her stomach. She held both hands up to her face and paled. Then she held them out for Dedge to see—ugly red welts blistering both palms.

"Ya should have stayed out of the way."

He threw the cane back into his right hand and came at WC again, holding it like a switch.

"Ya nasty little bantam, see what ya did."

"You'll pay for that, old man."

WC retreated to the door.

"Ya better run outside where I can't catch ya."

"I'm not going anywhere. Come and get me, if you can."

Dedge closed within arm's length. WC faked left and side stepped right, beyond the old man's outstretched hand.

Della continued to gaze in disbelief at her hands.

WC scampered to the far end of the room calling, "Here I am. Come on and get me." He pressed himself against the bedroom door.

Dedge followed, tromping the cane down and hopping after it. He spread his arms, funneling WC toward the corner.

WC pointed behind Dedge.

"Yeah, Ma, crack him."

Dedge flinched and glanced behind him. No one was there.

WC dodged around him and retreated against the kitchen chair at the end of the table. He stood his ground as Dedge's looming presence pinned him there. Small, defenseless, he focused on the old man's throat as the knob slid slippery up and down his neck with each curse spit at the boy.

"Look at me!" Dedge pulled the cane back.

"Try and hit me, old man."

WC covered his nose behind his fists and began dancing side to side—meager knuckles curled loose and relaxed.

"Come on, see if you can hit me."

Dedge lowered the cane, momentarily baffled. He did not know quite what to do about the bouncing fearlessness before him—laugh or smash it.

WC dropped his guard and stood still. "You know, you've never hurt me once in all these years, ol' Dedge."

"Is that right? Well, we'll see about that."

He ripped the cane above his head, snarled, and slashed it toward the boy's unprotected neck.

Della screamed as the cane cut the air.

WC ducked below the level of the chair.

The whistling cane chopped onto the chair's back and flew from Dedge's hand. It struck a rafter and clattered by the door. WC crawled under the table and emerged from the other end to see Dedge holding his wrist, rocking from pain and hollering.

"Ya broke my hand! I'll kill ya for that."

He showed it to Della.

"Look what he's done. The little devil broke my hand." He collapsed into the chair hugging his hand and moaning it hurt.

"Serves you right, you mean old thing."

"Stop it! Both of you!"

WC saw her wince, hold her hands before her and stare helplessly at them. He glared at the old man as he beat the table with his good hand and cursed Della for her lack of sympathy.

"You'll not whip me anymore—not without paying a price yourself. You hear me, old man?" He edged around the table and leaned into the man huddled around his injured hand.

"You're lucky I don't yank off your arm and beat you with the bloody end for burning Ma."

Della mourned, "Lord, no, please."

"I hate you, Dedge. I hope you die, so I can spit on your marker."

Dedge's hand shot up and backhanded WC on the face.

It staggered him back and he wiped a rip in his lip and tasted blood.

"Didn't hurt. You never know how to hurt me."

The cane was lying in the light of the screen door. WC scooped it up and carried it like an ax back toward the table.

Della stepped in his way. "Put his cane down. Don't be taking it up yourself."

"He hit me and has to pay. I'll chop him to pieces."

"Give me the man's stick." She held out her hand.

He flicked a look into her face. "No."

He stared hard at Dedge. "He burned you. I'm not letting him get away with that."

"Put it in my hand. I mean it; right now." She snapped her fingers for his immediate response.

The expectant palm before him, disfigured by a blister, represented her pain and authority. She deserved to be obeyed, but he could not give up the cane. There was the oath he had committed to: "hurt me, and it will cost you." The old man had to pay.

"I won't do it."

He threw open the screen door, jumped down the porch steps and flung the cane, wind milling, into the air. It landed and sprung against the rail fence.

He marched back into the house. "If you care anything about that ol' prop of yours, you'll find it on the fence by the drive up."

"Go get it, boy, and bring it back. Do what I tell ya." Dedge stood.

Della walked from them and turned to the counter at the sink. She cut fresh slices of pork.

"You're not my daddy and I've had enough of you."

Dedge spat a length of dark juice at WC, spattering his bare foot.

The boy grinned it was nothing and wiped it on the back of his pant leg.

The old man grinned back. He fingered a lump of tobacco from under his lip and slung it in a line across WC's neck.

"Boy, you ain't nothing but the bottom of an outhouse."

"And that's good enough for me."

WC dug a slice of pork from his pocket and gnawed at one end. "Not too bad," he said and tossed the leftover toward Dedge.

"You ought to try some yourself. It was fit for pigs you said."

He ducked as the meat flew into the screen, and then turned for the door, picking up the egg basket as he went out.

"I won't be needing breakfast. I'll leave the egg basket squatted out on the porch."

CHAPTER TWO

THE SHOES

The collisions between the boy and the old man took place all too often now, but WC went about his chores as if nothing had happened. The routine of the work relieved him of thinking about the fight. There were other matters to concentrate on, one at a time, to save life and limb. Survival was how he understood chores.

"Besides," his daddy's wisdom had taught him, "worrying on something never got anything done. Most times you know what's right to do—you just have to step out and do it."

Whenever his tongue reached up and touched the split, puffed lip, it was all the facts he needed to know about the making of a decision. It was time for him to take a step. Something had to change. It was too dangerous to allow things to continue as they were.

He had collected eggs, fed and watered the mules and Dedge's horse. He had sloshed mash into the garbage bucket, stirring the potato peels, egg shells, and carrot tops swirling into the thickening soup. Then he lugged it to the pen, just outside the feed trough, and dumped through the fence. The pigs, with upturned, snorting snouts, shoved and bit and squealed. There was no politeness in a pig sty and some of the slop dashed off their hoggish heads onto WC's pant legs. It did not bother him—it would dry off.

The chickens were next. He cast a bucket of corn to them. They flocked to each handful, preferring to quarrel at each new feast, rather than finishing the last. No matter how he scattered the kernels, they fought in a hungry mob, pecking and flying at each other, trampling the feed. He guessed it gave them reason to scratch in the dust later, finding nuggets to treasure.

WC had an inescapable sympathy toward runts, and every litter of pigs seemed to have one that was squeezed out of the feeding. At the end of chores, when feeding ear corn to the hogs, he did more than unload his pail over the rail. He tossed ears to a corner, trying to lure the bigger animals away, so as to guarantee the runt a sure cob of its own. But it was too slight and easily bumped away; left squalling fruitlessly below the thief's slobbering mouth.

Today, however, WC decided it was going to get its fair share. He climbed over the rail into the greasy muck and trapped the puny thing in a corner. He carried it out as it kicked and squealed torturously and set it on the ground. It bawled until WC shucked a handful of kernels off an ear and laid them in front of him. It greedily filled its mouth, crunching the grain, looked over both shoulders for the expected rush, grunted with self pleasure and filled its mouth again. It rolled the cob sniffing at it.

WC sat in the red clay dust with his legs hugged up to his chest. He rocked on his bottom and his bare toes squeezed the dirt into dry silky worms between them. The piglet's safety pleased him.

"You're mighty stingy with thanks, Pee Wee." WC nudged its side and Pee Wee yelped back in annoyance.

"Don't expect me to favor you out every day, though. You're a sorry sight for sure, but you best be figuring how to make it on your own."

WC rested a few moments longer, watched the kernels disappear off the red cob and listened to the snuffling animal fill its belly. Little Pee Wee finished the cob and began exploring, rooting for something more. WC picked him up sadly and set him back inside the pen.

"Sorry, little friend, but I have work to do."

It hurt to see the stunted creature freeze with fear among its own kind. In a form of revenge, WC studied all the porkers, selecting the ones most likely to be butchered out at summer's end. Finally, he picked up the pail, walked away and turned his back on whatever life went on inside that fence.

He went to the river branch to wash up, and on the way back he passed Dedge's cane still leaned upside down against the stone wall. The old man's Adam's apple and his mother's blistered hands flashed back to him. But then mangy ol' Gabriel ran up, perched on the man's rotten old stick and flapped arrogantly. In a poetic display of justice, the old rooster turned parallel to the cane, settled himself, quivering, and drained dirtiness onto the handle and into the dirt.

Gabriel crowed belligerently, "Err, er,er, er,er, er, errrr." He bounced down, strutted before all creation and ran off to more mischief.

"Exactly my feeling," WC smiled in agreement. "Couldn't have said it any better, you old flock of feathers."

He pulled another slice of the blackened pork from his pocket and bit off a piece. He could not think he had done anything wrong in the house: stood his place against the man's meanness, that was all. How could his mother fault him for that? Even if she did, he could not let that weaken or confuse what he knew he had to do now. To put it off meant someone would be hurt seriously, and his mother's burns were bad enough. It was time. Leaving home was a decision that had been waiting to be made. His mother would not only argue against it, she would forbid it.

To go against his mother he not only had to trust the rightness of his decision, he would have to be ruthless in his determination. He would have to have the same heartless passion he used whenever he attacked work. Where some people went at work timidly, pecking around its edges, and others slunk away from it, ignoring it and heaping it upon someone else, WC went at it with the frenzy of a barbarian at war. His only concept of conquering work was to vanquish it, massacre it with ferocious energy, taking no prisoners. Now, faced with telling his mother he would be living life on his own, he needed that same ferocity of conviction within himself.

He worried the old man would take his spite out on his mother. Though there was not much time left before his walk to school, he had to know what was happening inside the house. He flipped a pail over beneath the kitchen window and stood on it to see inside. He was relieved to find his mother calmly leaned against the counter, holding her hands across her chest. Her palms were wrapped in white cloth, but her fingers looked puffed and shined from butter she had spread on the blisters. Dedge sat rock stiff in the kitchen chair. An ocean swelled between the two of them. In front of Dedge, however, was a package wrapped in brown paper tied with white string.

WC stepped down and sat against the house.

"Old Dedge has been to the store," he thought. "Ma said she had a surprise for me. That must be it."

He wondered what might be in the bundle and squeezed his mind to crawl inside the paper.

"Too big for a hunting knife. I hope it's not clothes." He despaired at the idea, but then his hopes rose with a new thought.

"She knows I want a hat like daddy used to wear. The kind with a wide brim all the way around the crown and a silky ribbon band circling it. I would wear it all the time. She knows I'd like one; maybe that's what it is."

He stood on the pail and looked again. It did not have the right shape and he slipped back down disappointed and heavy as his enthusiasm evaporated.

His mother had given him his daddy's hat the day Sonny Lee was buried. She placed it on his head just as his daddy had done at the end of each day. She said, "He would want you to have this." But he did not wear it long, because he could not imagine his daddy without it—anywhere. He put it in the coffin over his father's hands, ran away and hid.

He watched the funeral from behind an oak tree, snapping off pieces of bark and sailing them angrily away. His daddy had broken out in spots, raised a fever and died. That was more than three years ago, and no matter how he tried to choke the memory off, he still felt the pain and emptiness.

He wiped one sleeve under his running nose and the other sleeve under his eyes. It surprised and shamed him that he should have tears—it had been long ago since the last time.

"Dry up, you big baby," he said to himself. "There's nothing so bad you can't stand up to it and spit. So get up you ol' fanny, and get to school."

WC started for the front of the house, but as he turned the corner he walked right into Gabriel. The startled rooster squawked back momentarily, then recovered its natural cussedness, spread its neck feathers and charged. WC kicked the first rush away and received a vile pecking on his bare foot.

Handling and controlling the bigger animals came easy to WC. Joe and Kate, the mules, and Tom, Dedge's horse, would do anything for him. You could train them. But chickens were altogether something different. There was no place to hold them. They were all feathers, part running, part flying.

He told his mother once, "Their heads are too small for brains enough to know gratitude for feeding. You can't sweet talk a chicken—you have to bully them."

After suffering the indignity of being tumbled in the dust, the rooster came back at WC with intensified fury, its wings throttling the air and its beak open for piercing and tearing. WC struck it solidly in the head with the pail. It rolled to the side, but was at his feet before he could swing the bucket again. It stabbed at his legs, until WC finally kicked it against the house. Then once again the deranged animal came for him. WC caught it by the neck and held it away from his body. Gabriel, unable to use the beak, dug with vicious toenails, and WC's arm was slashed. The animal screeched wildly, flapped and kicked frantically. It was a blur of feathers at the end of WC's bleeding arm.

No matter how hard its neck was squeezed, the rooster could not be brought under control. Before another thought could stop WC's hand, he whipped Gabriel into a circle and snapped his wrist down. The head popped off. The body flopped to the ground, flapping and flinging blood. But the head was still in WC' hand—calm and open-eyed.

WC threw it to the ground and mashed it with his foot, disgusted and burning at what had happened.

"See what you made me do, you blamed ol' mean thing!"

Feathers whooped against feathers, as the carcass struggled to stand or fly. But it could not balance without the head and beat itself again and again back into the billowing red dust. It was queer to see such tumultuous energy without a cry clamoring with it, and WC could stomach no more. He grabbed Gabriel's legs, the violent plunging ebbing, and carried him to the front of the house. By the time he tossed the dusty mass of feathers up on the side of the porch, the body barely quivered. WC hated to see dying.

"Most things went in a pitiful struggle," he thought. "Everything hangs on to life with devilish stupidity: pigs at slaughter, cottonmouth snakes chopped in half with a hoe, coons and rabbits hunted from the woods—even people. Like Ma marrying Dedge to hold on to land."

WC pulled up his sleeve and cocked his arm to see what damage had been done. The flesh was torn and ugly, but not deep. It stung and certainly needed to be cleaned and dressed. He called to his mother.

Della carried his lunch pail as she came out the door, the wire handle buried in the bandaging on her hand. She stopped when she saw the headless rooster and lifeless curled feet.

"Oh, Lord, what have you done?"

"I cricked off ol' Gabriel's head, can't you see? Didn't mean to do it, but he was fighting me and I couldn't get him to stop. I'm sorry, Ma, but he was too mean. You couldn't even cross the yard if he was in it. You had to go the long ways around or fight him off."

Dedge tottered out. "Killed the rooster, hey? That's not very smart, when it's the only one on the place." He sat in the porch rocker with the brown bundle in his lap.

"Don't worry yourself about it. I'll find a way to replace him."

"What did you do to your arm?" Della gasped. "My Lord, let me see." She examined the welts and gashes, while he told her about smashing Gabriel with the bucket and not even slowing the little beast down.

"You might look at my foot and my legs. He pecked me pretty good down there, too." He climbed on the porch and pulled his pant legs up for her to see.

"WC, that's awful. Looks like he nipped a piece of meat out every time he hit you. It could become infected and needs to be cleaned." She bustled inside.

As the door closed, Dedge began rocking the chair. "Be a terrible thing to have yer arm and leg fester and drop off," he sniveled.

WC turned his back and sat on the side of the porch, swinging his legs in the air.

"Well, if ya have nothing to say, go get my cane."

WC squinted at the green hills galloping against the blue horizon. The colors softened and blurred into a gentle, curving line. He closed his eyes completely and held the image calmly.

"I don't think I'll be doing that this morning."

"Ya don't?" Dedge said with pretended surprise, and then growled. "Well I'm telling ya to get it."

The colors behind WC's eyes faded to black and a slight pressure began to build in the bottom of one of his feet.

"I just killed the meanest, toughest thing on this place, old Dedge. You think I ought to be afraid of you?"

Clearly now, he could feel Gabriel's head mashed under his foot.

"Naw, you're nothing to worry about. You'll have to get your own cane, and let me tell you, you're in for a treat when you pick it up."

Della returned with a pan of warm water, soap and a towel. WC scooped handfuls of water and let them cascade down his arm. Once the wounds were cleansed, Della doused them with kerosene.

"I'm not going to bandage that arm. Keep that sleeve rolled up and let the air get to it. Don't get it dirty; that would be the worse thing you could do."

The rocker lurched, Dedge grunted slightly, and a brown parcel lumbered through the air and landed clumsily on the porch with a hollow "THUNK." It rolled to a halt in front of WC.

"There ya go boy, open it up," Dedge invited. "Before ya go to school, ya'll need them."

It could not be good, WC thought, the old man was entirely too anxious. He was on the edge of enjoying himself.

"Oh, Custer, that's not how I wanted to give it to him." Della walked half way to Dedge. "That's so crude, throwing his present around like that."

WC still could not guess at its contents. The sound it made against the planking of the porch was solid and heavy, so it was not clothes. Maybe an anvil.

"What's it for, Ma? Why am I getting a present?"

She held her hands out toward WC and returned to him, the bandaging soaked and loose, unraveling. "You needed them, since you grew out of the old ones and they blistered your feet," she said smiling.

"Shoes? A new pair of shoes?" He looked gratefully at his mother, past her hands, at her smile.

He had not had a pair on for months. Even before finally giving up the old ones, he had gone the entire winter cramming his feet into them and suffering foot cramps.

"Open them up," she said, and stooped down beside him.

He stuck his finger into a puny rip that the roughness had opened and began tearing the paper away. It came off in long brown sheets, rolling the contents over and over, tantalizing WC and his mother. Then the footwear tumbled free.

WC sagged away and left them in the tangle of white store string. He would not touch what he saw. Della, too, was appalled.

"Brogans," he said contemptuously. "Hard ol' brogans, stiff as boards." He had not seen such a quantity of leather except on an entire cow.

He poked one toward Della. "What am I suppose to do with this? Hitch it up to the mules and plow new ground?"

Della snatched the shoe up, stood, and turned it on Dedge. "These are not what I sent you to buy. You know they're not made for a boy's feet."

Dedge rocked easily in the chair. "No, they're made for men. They'll last a long time and big enough to grow into."

"You know he won't wear them. You want to humiliate him, that's all. I should know better than to trust you to do something."

"The boy thinks he's a man. Let him fit into a man's shoe."

"Where are the laces? There's not even any laces in them."

Dedge lifted a shoe and crossed it over a knee.

"Yeah, I needed new ones myself." He tossed a wad of old laces to Della.

"Those are good enough for him. Or, if not, he can use the string from the wrapping."

"It's beyond imagination, Custer Dedge, that anyone could dream up such spite to use on a boy."

"Ma." WC slung the pan of water on the ground and hopped off the side of the porch. "I'm not wearing them."

Dedge rocked forward. "Yes, ya are. They're bought, paid for, and no taking them back. Ya'll wear them and be thankful."

"I won't ever wear them hard old things."

Dedge stood and sent the chair thumping into a fit.

"Della, run out to the fence and get my cane."

She threw the shoe to the floor by its mate and took a collision course for Dedge. Her voice rumbled for his hearing only.

"He will not be forced to wear those shoes to satisfy some ache you have for meanness." She leaned closer still, forcing him to pull back.

"For the life of me, I cannot imagine how I ever allowed myself to–" She turned away abruptly. "Ohhh, it's too late for that now."

"WC." She waited for him to turn his face up to her. "I don't expect to see those shoes on your feet."

She nodded at him, picked up the stiffened rooster, and turned to the house. As she opened the door and met Dedge's threatening glare she stopped.

"Do your worse, but I'm not making him wear those brogans."

She called back over her shoulder, "Don't forget your lunch pail." The door slammed behind her.

WC set the brogans together, netted them in the string and slung them over his shoulder. He caught the lunch pail's handle and started for school, swinging it lightly back and forth.

Dedge dragged to the front edge of the porch. "Ya better have them shoes on yer feet when ya come home."

WC began whistling.

"Throw my cane back up here."

WC stopped at the split rail fence and set the pail and brogans down. He kicked the cane aside and picked up the shovel laying there. He dangled the brogans from the handle, rested the shovel over a shoulder, grabbed the pail and set off for school again, swinging his lunch pail and whistling.

* * * * *

Out of sight of the house, on the downward slope of Hickory Hill, a good seventy, eighty paces off the road, WC sang to himself and dug a hole behind a shrubby oak. It was two hymns deep—all four verses. He began humming a dirge and scooped the shovel under the brogans. He held their weight over the grave until the tune was completed, and then dumped them with no further ceremony. They spilled to the bottom of the trench, toe over sole.

"Not so tidy," he said to himself. "But as much trouble as I care to go to."

He pitched shovelfuls of red dirt over them and spoke parting words with reverential gravity.

"Ashes to ashes, dust to dust, and manure to manure."

He sang a verse of <u>When The Roll Is Called Up Yonder,</u> while raking the remaining dirt pile onto the cavity. He left the shovel under the brush, picked up his pail and started for school, chewing on a slice of side pork. He turned back once to see if everything appeared natural. It did.

"Rest in peace, you ol' brogans."

CHAPTER THREE

THE DEED

Beyond the small congregation of trees that gave the name to Hickory Hill, a grassy meadow crowned across the slight rise and sloped down to the taller weeds and softer woods that grew along the banks of the river. It darted with songbirds.

WC jogged a short cut through it to meet the road again at the small, hardly distinguishable, pioneer cemetery. Only the collapsing rail fence and the few visible grave markers told the story of early settlers laying family members to rest, giving rise to the site. WC's father, grandparents and sister, who had died being born, lay among them. Engraved hickory slabs marked their places. WC stopped beside his father's that read—

Wallace Lee Thomas
Sonny 1869-1907

The nickname, Sonny, came from Wallace's mother, who began calling him that as a child because of his "sunny disposition." It stuck, and everyone used it, linking it with his middle name.

Sonny Lee took WC out to work with him from the time the little guy could walk. The man loved to laugh and talk: demonstrating this tool to the child, telling that story about the weather and animals, explaining the different kinds of trees and soils. According to Della, "WC couldn't squeeze a word in," and never learned to say much, but before long, he could stake and chain the goat by himself, sharpen the kitchen knife to a razor's edge, and bridle Kate and Joe and lead them like pets.

WC knelt beside the grave site and dug out a weed offending his father's grassy plot. He tossed it away.

"Hey, Daddy. Remember you told me to 'never kick a rock for breaking a plow point? I would only hurt my own foot?' Well, it's exactly what I've been doing with ol' Dedge. And you were right; it doesn't make me feel any better. So I'm taking that advice, but I'll be leaving home to do it. Ma will be all right. She'll be better off, I suspect, without me there to rile up the old man."

He pressed his lips together, squeezed his eyes closed and tried to remain still and quiet for a few moments. He could not, however, halt the thought that he, too, would be among the "dearly departed"—no longer of his home.

He stood and looked up the road. "I don't know what's going to happen, but one thing's for sure—my foot is not going to hurt anymore. It's not worth it."

He lingered those few minutes, and then began striding for school, remembering how things went bad after his daddy died. Thinking about the funeral, with all the people singing and praying, broke him into a trot, and he began replaying memories, hot and real.

There was the particular image of Mr. Alvin Ray Dedge, Custer's older brother. It was a substantial show of nerve to join his baritone voice with those singing there, considering how he had taken advantage of Sonny Lee and the family. Della did not veil her feelings when he tried to sympathetically pat her hands at the close of the service. She pulled them behind her back and would not even look at him. He tugged his hat on his head and strode off muttering to himself.

Alvin Dedge came to own the Thomas farm when Sonny Lee was forced to put it up for sale to pay debts he had incurred experimenting with rice production. With Dedge's influence and power, provided by more money than anyone else had, he was able to discourage other bidders and get the Thomas' family land for much less than its value. However, Sonny Lee and the family were allowed to stay on and work the land as sharecroppers. It was kindness, Alvin Dedge told them, but they soon learned what everyone else indebted to him already knew: owing Mr. Alvin was a sorry saddle to sit on.

Sonny Lee tolerated the new life without complaint, but Della hated the way the man used their neediness. Whenever he took advantage of her husband, she wandered from her usual quiet Christian acceptance of life and questioned, argued, and complained.

Once, when Alvin Dedge demanded two new acres be opened for crops, it left them clearing and pulling stumps in the winter. That following fall, everything produced by Sonny Lee and the family was shared half and half with Mr. Alvin, except the bumper crop of sweet potatoes grown on the two new acres. He took them all. Only a few bushels for personal use were allowed for the family—none for the turning into cash. Della was so angry, she took an armload of potatoes off Mr. Alvin's wagon and strew them into the yard, saying, "If you want every potato on the place, you pick them up yourself." Sonny Lee had to physically carry her inside the house to keep her from unloading more potatoes. WC followed them and stood at the door, while his father sat at the table holding his mother on his lap.

"I reckon I'm the luckiest man alive, with someone like you on my side. Woman, taking a chance like that! That man would run you over if you were to take two cents from his pocket."

"You shouldn't let him treat you like that."

"You're right. WC, get me my gun. I'll shoot him."

"No, say something." she held his shoulders and shook him.

"What do you want me to say?"

He raised Della from his lap and stood. "Here's the latest news from our Alvin Dedge. Next year, we get to share in the two new acres, if we free up two more acres this winter."

"Two more!" she gasped. "Not again."

"And he says that if I figure I can't do it, he knows another man and family who can and would be more than grateful."

He walked to the window at the sink and looked out. "Now what would you have me say to that?"

"It's not right. He shouldn't be allowed to do that."

Sonny Lee looked back dismally. "What are we supposed to do? Move into a log?"

He hung his head, shook it in disbelief, then looked up and WC, for the first time, saw the smile, the ready humor—the hope stripped off his father's face.

"We're trapped right now. Can't see any way clear."

No one moved—husband and wife, each held their pain and thoughts, unable to cross the floor and take the other's suffering in their arms. Alvin Dedge's wagon, heavily loaded, creaked away into the distance.

WC was five then, old enough for impressions to construct themselves into a prejudice against Mr. Alvin. Every time he showed up, for whatever reason, WC's first response was to spit.

One week to the day after Sonny Lee was buried, Alvin Dedge drove his buggy into the yard. A young reckless rooster attacked the wheels until they came to a stop in front of the porch. WC stood at the bottom of the steps cradling an armload of stove wood.

"Where's your ma?"

WC shrugged and spit into the dust.

"Find her for me; I need to talk to her."

Della appeared in the doorway. "Is there something I can do for you?"

"Just came by to offer again how sorry I am that Sonny Lee was lost to you all. Terrible misfortune"

He began climbing out of the buggy.

"Where are you going? Why are you getting out?" Della stepped from the door and let it slam.

Mr. Alvin hesitated, looked at her, and then heaved himself the rest of the way to the ground.

"Well, I have a few matters to discuss with you. Can we go inside, like civilized people?"

"I believe we're fine—just as we are." She held the door open.

"WC. Take the wood inside."

"I believe I'm fine—just as I am."

"Don't sass me! Do as I say," she snapped.

Alvin Dedge looked at the sky and smiled, moving his feet. He had a deep appreciation for power in all its forms.

WC sulked and considered just dropping the wood. But that would embarrass his mother and create a scene to be enjoyed only by the unwelcomed Mr. Alvin. A better thought would be to dump the entire load on top of the man's smug, toe-tapping feet. He did the best thing, however, and carried it into the house, where he heard Della tell the man not to come on the porch; she would come down. WC hurried back out and stood leaning against the corner porch post watching the grown ups at the back of the buggy.

Della's hands were fisted on her hips and she was glaring into the distance.

Alvin Dedge found it easier to speak to his shoes than to her granite form. "I didn't mean right this minute. You and the boy can stay on until spring."

"Until spring? What then?"

"I'll move another family in to take over."

"Look here, Alvin Dedge, this is Thomas land, and we—"

"No, it's not, either."

They stood squared off to each other.

"You may have bought it—stole it, more like it—but it's Thomas life and death that's paid for every rock thrown aside and weed turned under. Who really owns it? We do. And we had every hope to get ahead and buy back what was really ours."

Alvin Dedge could not match that passion and again examined his shoes and shook his head.

"That won't happen, Della. Now or later. It won't happen."

"WC and I can run this farm ourselves."

He laughed and began shaving a toe at the hard red clay.

"We can."

"I have an investment here and need positive assurance it will turn a profit." He looked toward the porch. "I can't expect a woman and a boy—what is he, four or five?"

WC blurted, "I'm six, mister."

"Hush, WC! Go on in the house," Della ordered.

He was not about to leave the spot he was standing on—no matter what was threatened.

"You don't know what my son is capable of. He worked beside Sonny Lee every day of his life. And this season, because of him, I never had to lift one finger to the farm work. He completely took my place."

Mr. Alvin dragged more clay into a pile. "I can imagine how hard you'd try. You'd break your backs at it, but I don't believe it's possible for a woman and boy to keep up with this farm. I stand to lose money."

"Give us the chance."

"You have kinfolk to take care of you. Your brother, Otis, he'd be proud to have you." He lightly tamped the heap of shaved dust.

Della crossed her arms. "Otis and all the rest have cares enough without taking us for burdens. Besides, it's not necessary. Leave us here next season and we'll have your shares ready for you, just like always."

Alvin Dedge looked at the small mound of soft red dust beside his shoe. He had wanted to be back in his buggy, on his way home by now. Why was she making this so difficult? She was always out of place with him, irritating.

On the spot, though, an idea began to emerge. It was possible something could be gained. He pulled off his hat, wiped his brow with a blue handkerchief, and watched their new rooster herd a trio of hens behind the house. He looked at Della.

"I can't believe I'm even thinking this. But tell you what I'll do. You and the boy—what's his name—" he nodded toward the porch, "can stay on. I'll send my brother over—you know Custer, don't you? He can keep track of your progress, maybe help out if you need it, and report to me any problems. Don't I know he needs some responsibility. It'll be good for him and may save you a place here. Who knows, maybe some day you will earn this place back. I'd let it go at a fair price."

Della shook her head and said, "We can manage without him."

She was completely aware of Custer's sour outlook on life, and the spiteful relationship existing between the brothers. Stories circulated the region about their actual fist fights and legal battles over inherited property. Custer's injury was legendary throughout the county.

Young brothers argued over whose turn it was to shoot the gun. They called each other names. Then shoving led to grabbing, and grabbing led to wrestling. One boy punched the other in the face. The gun was picked up, fired and the other boy was crippled the rest of his life. Alvin maintained it was an accident; he was not aiming to hit his brother—just shooting close to scare him. Custer believes he did it on purpose and took all his life's chances from him. Unlike Alvin he never completed school, ran away from home, lived a vagrant life, and returned seventeen years later to take advantage of his dependency on what he called, "My brother's good looks and good luck."

They may have lived under the same roof, but no love was lost on either of them. Della wanted no part of their feud.

"Your brother has better things to do than watch over us."

"No, it would be an important, productive way for him to protect the family interest here. I like the idea."

He set the hat back on his head, tipped it off his brow and shoved his hands in his pockets.

"It would be a waste of your brother's time."

"Well, that's the way it's to be, Della. It's how I want it."

He looked so pleased and puffed, rocking on his feet. She knew it was wasted breath to argue further.

"If that's the way you want it, after the years you never had to worry about your 'investment' here, I reckon we'll work around your brother. Now, if your business is finished, I'll thank you to leave."

His hands came out of his pockets. "You're acting pretty high up, woman."

"I buried my husband a week ago. He always bent to you without a word of disagreement. If I have to see your side of things, it does not have to be with smothered feelings."

He pointed a stubby finger into her face and shook it near her nose. "It wouldn't be wise right now, to be stupid."

"You leave my ma alone!"

WC yelled and leaped from the porch. He tried to tackle the man, but Mr. Alvin held him off by his shoulders. WC growled, kicked at his shins and swung wildly.

"This is some wildcat you bred," he laughed.

"I'm not a wildcat! And my name is not 'what's his name.' "

Della stooped and held WC thrashing in her arms. "Turn loose of my son, Mr. Alvin. He won't hurt you now."

She held him tightly, shushing him, speaking soothingly. "Be still, Son. We've got to let this big ol' man get on his way home. There's people waiting for him—a brother breathless for his return."

He began to calm and she petted his back.

Alvin Dedge strode past them, obstructed by the tenderness, toward his buggy.

"We'll give you a try this spring, and see how it turns out. I'm demonstrating good faith here, Della Thomas, I hope you appreciate it."

He raised a foot to the buggy step and turned back. "I'll be sending Custer around a little before time to break ground."

Della stood and pushed WC behind her.

"We'll be on the lookout for him," she said, as if she had just been warned of an escaped lunatic.

Mr. Alvin raised a vaulting look at her. He was tempted to teach her a lesson about female arrogance and clear her off the land with no further delay. But this opportunity to involve Custer was a glowing possibility, too priceless to waste on unchecked emotions.

He flashed a quick smile. "You do that. You be ready." He pulled himself up onto the seat and reached for the reins.

"Hey, mister," WC called as he stepped around his mother's skirt. "Wait a minute."

"What's on your mind, boy?"

WC walked below him, staring up. "My name's Warren Carl Thomas, since you don't know."

"You're a real snot-slinger, aren't you, Warren Carl Thomas? I hope you can farm better than you can fight."

"You'll see, mister."

Alvin Dedge laughed, then called back over his shoulder to Della, "When Custer gets here, I think you all will be about right for each other."

He jerked the horse's head around and slapped its rump with the reins. The buggy bounced away with the young rooster, Gabriel, chasing behind.

Mother and son watched it turn at the bottom of the road. Della rumpled WC's hair. He covered up and she smiled at him.

"You better be watching your nerve, son."

"You too," he said.

* * * * *

By the time Custer showed up in the spring, they were well into plowing. With favorable weather and determined work from dawn until dusk, they were ahead of the season and looking forward to an early planting. But Custer, without any discussion, broke open the two smallest fields by himself. Della argued they would do it and for him to leave well enough alone, but he kept at the plow saying they were lucky he was there to help.

WC said it was the poorest plowing he had ever seen, not nearly deep enough, and had to redo much of it.

After that Custer did not come often, and when he did he came late, found the shade and left early. He was, however, an appreciative diner, always quick to praise Della's cooking and sometimes bringing food he would like prepared.

They never saw Alvin Dedge, until he showed up to inspect his share of the late potatoes. He was unusually subdued and uncertain of himself. Della again ushered him away from the sanctity of their porch to the rear of his buggy.

"I have to say the two of you did all right, this year. I didn't think it was possible." He started to good naturedly pat her shoulder, but the sudden rigidity of her body made him hold off and rub his hands together instead.

WC watched from the porch steps. He was secluded among sacks of sweet potatoes indiscriminately placed throughout the porch and steps. Though Della had cautioned him to stay out of the way and keep any thoughts to himself, he lurked there, restrained, but ready and unafraid.

"Custer says you did better than any woman and boy could have done, but that without his help you would have been short two or three fields."

"He said that?"

"Yes. He said you came up short, but real close."

Della wondered about Alvin Dedge's apparent discomfort. For some reason he could not look her in the eyes, but stared off at the field beyond the rail fence. And his face was freshly shaven and lilac scented the air between them.

"Yeah, he told me he admired your spirit and determination."

She moved to stand in front of his gaze.

"Let me tell you something. We would have done all the fields ourselves, but Mr. Custer plowed those fields before we had the chance. What he did was not needed. He never touched a cultivator nor a hoe to those fields—we did it all after his miserable plowing. When he came, he sat and watched. The only time he joined us was to sit at meal time.

"Well, that's not the way I heard it." Their eyes met.

"I can't help how you heard it, but that's the truth. I'm telling you, we would have sweated every inch entirely ourselves, if left alone."

"But the flat out truth is you didn't do it all yourselves. And I'm sorry to say that has to show up in the sharing."

Della turned sharply away.

"It's what I've come to expect from you."

WC called out. "That man couldn't plow a straight line or hold his depth, if his life depended on it."

Della half turned and raised her hand in caution toward him.

"So what are you saying?" she asked Mr. Alvin. "What about those two fields, he said he did?"

"Well, you didn't earn the right but to one half of each of those fields, the best we figure. We don't feel the obligation to share what you did not work. It's only fair."

"My Lord." Della shook her head. "After your half of those fields we'd be left to share just over two acres of those potatoes, when WC toiled over ten." She pointed back at WC.

"I want you to know, that boy had to plow over what your brother had done. He harrowed those fields, worked them into hills, planted them, mulched them, and kept the bugs off— all by himself, while Mr. Custer enjoyed soda biscuits and molasses in the shade. If you want to take that away from the boy, I guess you will, but I want the truth of it in your conscience."

"Woman, you make everything harder than it should be. I gave you your chance here, and it didn't work out. Now, I'll have to make a change and bring in another family I know I can trust to do all the work."

"Another family? But we proved ourselves. We worked every inch you wanted."

"No, you didn't. But I won't argue with you, anymore."

He strolled several steps away jamming his hands into his front pockets.

Della watched him go past, but sensed he had more to say.

"So, Alvin Ray Dedge, when are we supposed to have our things out of here?"

"How would you like to stay?"

"Stay? You just said you were moving another family in."

Alvin Dedge turned and looked pathetically frightened: his eyes were wide and searching. He rubbed at his lips.

"My brother has feelings for you."

"What?"

He took his hat off, held it over his heart, and began circling it with nervous snatches of his fingers.

"His coming here every day was good for him."

"Every day?"

"He's told me what a fine woman you are." He suddenly felt a strain and crushed the hat.

“I had some blame in Custer’s being crippled, and I have dedicated myself to watching out for him ever since. I’d hate to see him pass up something he deserves and blame it on the accident he had when he was just a boy.”

He gave the poor hat a twist. “Coming here was good for him—you were good for him.” He closed his eyes, praying for help.

Della relieved him. “What are you talking about? He did not come here every day, and if he made you think we were—‘friendly,’ even held a conversation beyond ‘pass the beans,’ it would be a lie.”

“He has an interest in you.”

She laughed and shook her head.

“No.”

WC swatted Gabriel off the porch and sent him squawking around the side of the house with chunks of clay.

The tortured hat was again placed over Mr. Alvin’s heart.

“I’m speaking for Custer when I say he wishes to take up with you… Marry you.”

Della raised her arms toward heaven and laughed.

“He has marrying on his mind.”

“You may think it’s funny, but here’s the whole deal: take Custer on and marry him and you can stay on the farm. If you don’t, I’ll be asking you to leave.”

WC called out. “That man is too old for Ma.”

Della pointed at the door.

“WC, go in the house and keep still.”

He looked at Della and then at the man.

“Go on, do what I say. I’ll be all right.”

He backed to the side of the porch and hopped up to his seat.

"In the house, I said."

Alvin Dedge swung his hat impatiently in WC's direction.

"Go on, boy, do what your mother tells you to do. No one's asking for your two cents, so keep your trap shut."

WC rose leisurely, like a vine twining the porch post. He sauntered to the door, opened it wide enough to admit every animal on the farm and, without walking through, slammed it shut, as if he were closing the door to Hell. He scratched luxuriantly under his arm, before straddling a sack of potatoes above the steps.

Alvin expected Della to do something about his disobedience.

She smiled and shrugged at him.

"You should have left well enough alone."

"Be serious, you have a decision here, woman, and it needs your thorough attention. Will you have Custer or will you shake your things together and leave. That's the choice."

"He never showed interest in anything around here. Especially us. And I never held out any encouragement—you can bet on that."

"Don't puzzle over this one minute. He's all for the idea—100 percent. He likes you and the boy, and would do right by both of you."

He held the hat out toward her.

"In a way, he would have his own here, and carry some responsibility in the family business. All the way around, someone gets what they want."

"Oh, I see. And he would be out of your way. Is that it?"

She lifted her chin and arched her eyebrows.

"I believe I'll take until the spring to decide on such a generous offer as a match with Custer Dedge."

"No, you won't either. If we can't agree on this today, right now as we stand, I'll send a wagon back to pack your things and set them off somewhere outside Beebe. You can turn your shares into cash and maybe board up two or three months. But then you'd be at the mercy of family or strangers. Now, it wouldn't be a bit of difference to me. I'd have my profit."

Della watched him as he began reassembling the shape of the hat. He snapped the brim down, smoothed his hair and set the hat challengingly on the back of his head.

"There's no getting around it, I want my answer as I'm standing here."

WC dismounted the potatoes. "I'll get the packing started."

"Sit back down," Della commanded. "Keep still."

He grabbed a potato and rolled it between his hands, as he slowly made his way down the steps.

"Listen to me, Alvin Ray Dedge. You bring me a proposal from a man who has never shown any feeling, and I have certainly never advanced any myself. I am expected to decide between marrying such as Custer Dedge and making ourselves homeless for the winter. And, you expect me to do this at the twirling of a hat?"

Alvin Dedge held his arms out and shrugged. "Custer is not the issue here, Della. It's how badly you want to hold onto this land. My advice to you is don't give yourself so much to think about."

WC now stood beside his mother. She took her eyes from the man and turned them to the boy, putting her hands on his shoulders.

"Well, I would never agree to such a thing, unless I got something in return."

Mr. Alvin sensed the approach of a bargain. He began celebrating internally, knowing he was minutes from turning his buggy for home and telling Custer to pack up—he was moving to the Thomas' farm.

"Something in return? What would you have in mind?"

"Sonny Lee's daddy started this farm. There have been weddings here, births and burials. Thomas' sweat and flesh lies in this ground and it was Sonny's hope to pass it on to WC."

"Whoa, hold your horses now. You aren't thinking to take this farm from me, are you?"

"Let's think about your real issue, Mr. Alvin. How badly do you want Custer and his shrill twang at your supper table? Seems to me, you don't want to complicate the idea with too much thought."

"I can't give this whole farm to you. It's too valuable."

"I want the house."

"That's no problem. You can have the house."

"I want the five acres it sits on, the right of way from the road, and I want Hickory Hill and the cemetery."

"Now, you're getting greedy. You can have the house, the right of way, the cem--"

"Not an inch less. I want it free and clear. In my name, on paper, with your signature."

WC tossed the potato toward Mr. Alvin. He was startled and clumsy, but managed to catch it after fumbling it against his stomach. He sneered at the boy, then turned away, hefting the potato, weighing his thoughts.

Della interrupted them. "I need your answer now, as 'I'm standing here,' Alvin Ray Dedge. Or sure as water's wet, WC and I will move along, and you'll still have Custer underfoot, in your house, blaming you for every unhappiness."

She moved face to face with him. "I'll take Custer Dedge for you. But I get the house, the land, and the entire hill."

WC pulled at her dress. "Let's leave, Ma. That man spits too much."

She spun him around, swatted his bottom and pushed him toward the steps.

"I told you to go in the house!"

He pushed a sack over, spilling the potatoes to the ground, and ran out of sight around back.

Della returned to Alvin Dedge. "I mean every word. We'll leave, if I don't get the answer I want."

Suddenly, it was clear to him. Land, an offending woman, none of it mattered. To be rid of Custer was everything.

"You got your way," he told her. "You beat me."

"When will I see the papers?"

He smiled. "Tomorrow. I'll bring them by, if that's soon enough for you."

"No, I'll meet you at Fischer's Store at noon tomorrow. We'll have it witnessed properly."

"All right, then, noon." He climbed into the buggy, laughing. "I've done been outsmarted, Della. I hope you take to Custer's ways, I surely do. You got yourself a house and a husband. Both are yours till death do you part."

He laughed again as he turned the buggy.

Della ran alongside, holding onto the seat.

"There won't be any favors. You tell him that."

He looked down and laughed louder. She dropped her hand and stopped.

"No courtesies, you make it clear."

He twisted around and looked back, laughing harder.

"Oh, Della, the two of you will have to work that out. It has nothing to do with me."

CHAPTER FOUR

THE OUTHOUSE

WC heard the school bell ring through the woods as he was trotting the road curving with the river. When he finally rounded the trees, he saw the last of the students filing in the double doors. He slowed to a walk. Late already, he might as well catch his breath, stop at the pump and rinse some sweat and dust off, before sliding in next to Dutton Baker. It was going to be his last day at school, probably forever, and maybe he need not be remembered so aromatically.

Mr. Bell noticed WC the moment he came in, but did not interrupt his directions for the sentences he wanted copied from the board. WC kept his head down and padded to his row. As he turned in, he looked up and saw his cousin Tommy Irene across the aisle grinning at him, holding up three fingers and mouthing the words "Three whole days in a row."

"Thomasina!" Mr. Bell called to her. "Turn around and mind your own business."

"WC's here again."

"I see that. Take your seat, Warren Carl. I am always glad to see you."

"It's three whole days in a row. That's a record, ain't it, cousin? About to kill Mr. Bell and the rest of us with surprise."

"That will be enough, girl, unless you want to sit up here and see what I have in the corner."

WC could have killed her. There were many times he would have killed her over the years; she was so pesky. She tattled on everyone, bragged about anything, lied about everything; was stingy, hateful, freckled, red-headed and tough as alligator skin. The worst thing about her to WC was that she always wanted to be with him, and they got along like oil and water. But he could never really be mean to her, because with all her aggravation he knew and understood her life. Even as he had glanced over when she was told to sit down, he saw she was wearing overalls again. The only girl he knew ever to wear them to school. It was not her fault, though—it was about all she had. Aunt Clair and the kids were worse off than anyone WC knew. Still, Tommy Irene had the nerve to come to school most days. Her brothers did not. No one teased her any more about the clothes after the bloody noses she gave.

Mr. Bell, too, protected her feelings. He was a good man, slow to use the canes other teachers kept stored threateningly in a wicker basket beside the desk. WC thought he was happier in his job, more ready with a smile and a complement than any adult he had ever met. Because of the persuasiveness of that good humor and an unusual willingness to reason with his students, he had less need for striking the children or the ranting and raving other teachers used to bully the class' behavior and learning. It was for this reason alone, his teacher, that WC had come, this, his last day of school. Mr. Bell deserved to be told, face to face.

On this particular morning, WC had hardly heard or done a thing. He felt little necessity to apply himself to the work at hand, and mostly stared out the window—his mind blanked. The only idea his mind wanted to entertain was how to tell his mother he was leaving home. So when they were dismissed for lunch, he looked forward to time alone to give it his full attention.

"WC. Hey, WC, where you going?" Tommy Irene stampeded up to him.

"To eat my lunch."

"What did you bring?"

"I don't know. Where's your lunch?"

"Didn't want one."

WC knelt down, opened his pail, pulled out one biscuit that had been sliced, buttered and smeared with sorghum.

"Take this and one of these roasted potatoes."

Tommy turned her nose up. "If I wanted anything, I would have brought my own, Stupid."

He put everything back and started walking away.

"Wait a minute. I got something to tell you."

"Go pester someone else. I don't want you around right now."

"If you don't listen, you're gonna be in trouble."

She intercepted his path to the shade tree he intended to sit against. "Can I see that biscuit again?"

He lifted the lid and she reached in and took the biscuit and potato. He wondered if the family even had a brush at home—her hair was so dry and frazzled. They kept it cut short, almost to the shoulders, and it looked like it had been whacked off with a knife. The red color was pretty though, even ragtag and bobtail. Neglect, however, dulled it. But how could she help it?

"C'mon," she said, "let's sit down and eat together. I've got some news." Hungrily, she took a bite of the biscuit and began chewing. "Ummm," she sighed and closed her eyes.

"Dang it, Tommy Irene, I don't want to be bothered. I got thinking to do and need to be left alone." He moved around her, but she followed him like a wrinkle on a shirt.

"It doesn't matter where you go, because I'll sit where you sit. It's a free country."

"Oh, no, you won't." He turned from the woods and began running back toward the school.

She chased after him. “You’ll get in trouble, if you don’t go home with what I have to tell you. C’mon back here.”

He ran past the schoolhouse, along the side, behind it to the outhouse. Tommy saw him step inside and close the door. A mere door would not stop her and she did not hesitate to slam herself against it.

“You come out! You’re not gonna eat your lunch in there. It’s smells.” She began kicking and pounding on the door. “Open up.”

A voice hollowed by four close walls yelled out, “Go away. I’m doing my business in here.” Then, as an after thought Tommy heard WC say, “Oh no, the door—it’s not hooked.”

She could not resist the temptation to prove he was just hiding. She pulled the door knob lightly. A hinge creaked, and the door cracked open. But then it was caught up short.

“It is too hooked, you liar,” she screeched and shouldered against the door again.

WC laughed.

“You’re not doing anything; get out of there, before I tell.”

Mr. Bell raised the window at the back of the school and leaned out.

“Thomasina, come here. What in the world are you doing out there?”

“Oh, Mr. Bell, I was just about to tell you that WC’s hiding in the privy, and won’t let me in to go. He knows blamed well I have a weakness of the insides, and he’s just wanting to see me wet my pants. Tell him to get out, so I can go. He’s been in there forever. Please, sir." She squirmed before him painfully, gritting and squinting.

"Oh, for heaven's sake, girl, you'll live." He called out toward the outhouse. "Warren Carl? Are you in the outhouse?"

There was no answer.

"He's there, sir. You can trust me."

He gazed at her and took in a deep breath. "Yes, I am sure I can." Again he turned his attention to the isolated building of unmistakable purpose.

"If you are in there, son, I want you to come out and let this little girl relieve herself." There was no response. The teacher's voice toughened. "Do not make me come out there and get you."

"He doesn't mean to, sir, but he can get real stubborn sometimes. I can wait a while longer."

The door was suddenly kicked open and banged against the wall. WC stood in the opening, for all of heaven and earth to see, in his long johns. The overalls were bunched around his ankles. He fastened a button at the seat of his underwear, turned back to the platform, dropped a piece of paper into the hole and lifted his pants. Looking at the schoolhouse, he saw his teacher slumped at the window, shaking his head. Tommy's hands covered her mouth, and she was redder than her freckles.

He stepped out and complained, "I was just finishing. A person ought to have enough time for the privacy of throwing his paper away." He hooked the strap to his brass button and walked away.

Tommy had not gotten one ounce of satisfaction from her complaints—WC's infernal nerve had cheated her. She turned her finger covered face to Mr. Bell.

"I'm gonna tell Aunt Della."

"Yes, I'm certain you will," he said and pulled back inside.

Tommy saw WC turning the corner of the school and began running for him and shouting.

"Wait, wait. Let me tell you something."

Before she had run five steps, Mr. Bell's voice brought her skidding to a stop.

"Thomasina Irene Collins, come right back here!"

She hung her head, slung her shoulders, and stood under the window. He nodded at her, gathering patience, while she wondered what he wanted.

"It comes to mind, little girl, you had the need of nature a minute ago, and now I expect you will seek the privacy you so noisily won." He motioned toward the outhouse.

She cocked her head to one side and held up her hands claiming to not know what he was talking about.

"I think you best high tail it for the privy before you 'wet yourself.' "

Recognition flashed over her face and she smiled preciously.

"Oh, yes. Well, sir, I reckon I don't have to go so bad it can't wait till after I catch up with WC. My maw told me to tell him something real important."

"Seems to me you could not wait long enough for Warren to pull up his pants and throw his paper away before. I'm thinking you better go right now. What with that 'weakness of the insides' and all, we would not want you sitting in a puddle all afternoon. Go on, now."

"Shoot," she muttered and stomped to the dreaded building. She pulled the door away from the wall, and then before stepping up inside, she hollered, "He's done broke the door, Mr. Bell."

She took an exaggerated breath and then closed the door.

Mr. Bell grinned as he heard her complain, "I hate it in here. Aw, shoot fire, the seat's plumb wet all over."

* * * * *

All through the afternoon lessons, Tommy Irene was agitated. She would stand, wiggle, and tug at the seat of her overalls. Then she would turn and glare at WC. When she could catch his eye, he would gaze away with a blissful mixture of boredom and self-satisfaction. It nettled her that much more, and served only to increase the itchy unpleasantness of her behind. Finally, the fuse of her patience sputtered out, and she exploded into a zillion red stars.

Tommy Irene stood up and hollered, "Dad burn you, WC," and threw her pencil at her table top.

The dang thing skipped off her desk and took off like an arrow. It flew over Nancy Ilert in the row ahead, began to lose power, dropped, and then nestled point down, in the back of Gertrude Foster's hair. It wiggled there, a spent shaft in her dangling coils.

Every eye had turned to Tommy Irene's outburst and seen the amazing feat of the ricocheting pencil.

The physical laws and possibilities of such a wondrous accident would be the subject of many stories and jokes later. But for the moment, everyone was in awe of the fact; the pencil was quivering, sure enough, bisecting the center of some of the prettiest curls in all of White County.

Gertrude brought the gasping admiration to an end. She shot straight up and favored ears and air with the two most exquisite screams a six year old soprano could produce.

"A BEE-EEE! A BEE!" She was frantic. She moved out into the aisle and to the front of the room.

The class was stunned. Every mouth gaped, as she screeched back and forth below Mr. Bell's raised platform.

"It's stinging! Get it out! Please, help mEEEEE!"

Tommy Irene at first stood paralyzed by the wayward pencil and watched Gertrude with guilt and shame. But she recalled the real culprit and tromped back to WC's seat, and began slapping him around the head and shoulders. He balled up, taking cover under his arms.

"You're to blame for all this. You peed on the seat. You did it on purpose, and now I'm itching and scratching all day."

Mr. Bell, poor man, found himself the recipient of two howling catastrophes: Gertrude, below him, puncturing eardrums with her screaming, and Tommy Irene, toward the back, slapping the fool out of WC. And if that was not bad enough, the class came to life, adding to the pandemonium.

They cheered and laughed as Tommy Irene grabbed Dutton Baker by the collar and pulled him off his seat, so she could get a better whack at WC.

"Thomasina!" Mr. Bell shouted at her. "Sit back down, girl."

Gertrude suddenly stopped screaming and froze in place. All bodies shifted to her in unison.

With her hands not quite touching her hair, she pleaded for mercy.

"It's drilling into my head! Oh, Mama, get it out!" And she began a new level of desperate, daggering cries and sweeping across the floor.

The student's laughter was seismic, tremoring the entire room. Some of the children slapped their desks; while others pointed at the pencil or rocked to relieve their strained stomachs.

"Trudy, stop your screaming. Lord help us, you are going to take the whitewash off the walls."

At the back, Tommy Irene resumed punishing WC; attention rolled to the rear of the room.

"It's your infernal fault, if I'm in trouble." Slap. Whack. Kick. "You peed on the seat and I got me a rash." Slug. Pound. Pinch.

Mr. Bell finally stepped off the platform, into the center aisle, and called toward the farther rows.

"Thomasina, stop that! Get back to your seat"

Behind him Gertrude's blurring screams twisted him around.

"Trudy, what is tormenting you?"

Laughter turned to the back of the room stopped, shifted toward the front, and the howls sparked to life again.

"Girls! Both of you stop this minute!"

Neither one of them heard a word. Tommy Irene continued to pummel WC and Gertrude to deafen the hard of hearing. Their classmates were in heaven—heads swiveling from one magnificent recess moment to another.

Suddenly, though, Gertrude halted, arrested, stopped dead in her tracks and silent. Every eye turned to her and even Tommy Irene paused her abuse. The silence from Gertrude was deeply felt by all, appreciated, even glorious. She faced the room limp and spiritless.

Then, slowly, she rose up on her toes, spread her arms, arched her neck and began crowing. Actually crowing and flapping her arms. No one knew why and no one laughed.

Mr. Bell had to consolidate his problems. He wrapped Gertrude in one arm, which silenced and stiffened her from head to toe, positioning her arms into a soaring angle. He bore her to where Tommy Irene stood defiant, hands to her hips. He swept her into his other arm and headed for the front of the room.

Tommy Irene was anything but stiff. She was the insides of a clock gone wild—arms and legs, gears and springs, going every which way.

He stooped and set Gertrude down on one side and tried holding Tommy Irene's struggling on his other knee. The screaming blared again and was pitched above the scale. Trudy started to run off and Mr. Bell stretched and snatched her back by a loop of her sash.

"Take a breath, girl. Get you some air."

He held both of them—one girl with a wing span, screeching, the other tugging and spitting fire. It was monumental: a Thomasina Collins and Gertrude Foster Greatest Show on Earth.

Mr. Bell looked out into the devastated classroom. Students were draped over table tops laughing. Their eyes were wet, and rollicking tears had to be smeared from cheeks. You could have sold peanuts and fried fruit pies and not been the least bit out of place.

Mr. Bell held Tommy Irene close to him.

"Irene," he spoke into her ear. "Irene, I want you to calm down."

She bucked against his arm and tried to slide under it, never one to give up easily. But she was less committed to the escape. No one else called her Irene—just a girl's name Irene, except her Aunt Della.

"Let me go. I didn't do nothing. It's WC's fault."

"Listen to me," he urged. "I want you to look out at the classroom. Can you see everyone is laughing? You're making a spectacle of yourself."

She looked out into the room; embarrassment stung her little body. She threw her arms around Mr. Bell and hid her face. He covered her with his arm.

"I didn't do nothing. It ain't my fault," she wailed into his neck.

WC stood up and made his way into the aisle, confessing, "She's right, Mr. Bell, it's all my fault. I just meant to have a joke, Tommy Irene, I didn't mean--"

"Sit down, Warren," Mr. Bell snapped.

"No, sir."

"I said 'sit down!' "

The classroom went silent. Even Gertrude's screech subsided to a drone.

"Let me care for the little girls and then we'll worry about who's to blame," Mr. Bell continued to flash at WC. "Can you see the sense in that? Sit down, stand up or leave, I do not care. But I will not be interrupted while I help these children. Do you understand?"

WC hesitated, staring at the man with his arms full of tearful girls. The boy turned and left the building. Moments later, students by the windows heard the water pump handle squeaking up and down.

The man leaned to the littlest girl and spoke tenderly.

"Trudy, put your arms down. Put them down and look at me." He pushed wisps of hair back from her cheeks, and she turned to him.

"Tell me what has gotten into you, darling? What scared you?"

Her little mouth pouted, drooping into resigned sadness. She stared at him through tired, half-lidded eyes.

"Can you talk to me? Are you hurt?"

She nodded.

"Where? Where did you get hurt?"

She pointed at the back of her head. "A bee stung me. And I'll probably die."

Sputtered laughter broke out amongst some of the students.

"You all be quiet out there! She's scared to death and you want to laugh at her? Where in the world did you get your kindness from?"

All humor was gone now. Just two pitiful tragedies remained: one muffling sobs in her teacher's collar, the other dreamy and unbelieving.

"What do you mean, a bee stung you?"

"It landed on my head."

She tapped him on the arm. "And Mr. Bell?"

"Yes, darling."

"It's still there. I can feel it."

"Show me."

She turned her back to him, ducked her head and pointed.

There was the pencil, loosened somewhat, but captured in the twining of her tight curls.

"It's a pencil, Trudy."

"Sir?"

"You have a pencil stuck in your hair."

"It's not a bee?"

"No, darling. It's a pencil." He drew it out and showed it to her.

"See? It even has teeth marks bitten all over it."

Tommy Irene pulled away from Mr. Bell's neck and hic-cupped.

"It's mine, Trudy, and I'm sorry." She took it, grasped it into her fist, and resumed her place of moisture on the man's collar, hic-cupping.

The teacher patted and rubbed Tommy's back.

"Mr. Bell?"

"Yes, Trudy."

"My baby sister got stung by a bee real bad. She died."

"Baby Sally, yes, I remember. It was a real sad time for your family."

"I'm scared of bees."

"If you thought you were stung, it would just about drive you crazy."

"Sally's box wasn't as big as a cradle."

"She was still a baby, just starting to walk."

Gertrude looked out at the class and began picking at her dress.

"It was a pencil?"

Tommy Irene pulled away, gave it to Trudy and hid again.

"See," Mr. Bell said, "it was Thomasina's pencil."

He tested the point with the tip of a finger.

"To some people a pencil has a stinger. But let me tell you something—it does not work on pretty curls. And you have some of the prettiest I have ever seen."

Tommy Irene sobbed out from Mr. Bell's shoulder, "That's true. I wish my hair was as nice."

Gertrude smiled.

Mr. Bell lifted both girls up into his arms.

"I'm going to take the girls outside and we're going to wash our faces and have a conversation to brighten our spirits. You all will continue the lesson, behave yourselves, to permit us this necessity, will you not?"

"Yes sir," the class intoned.

He walked down the aisle, his stout shoes clomping rhythmically to Tommy Irene's hic-cups.

CHAPTER FIVE

THE GULLY

As life would have it, Tommy Irene sure enough did have something important to tell WC. She had a letter from his Aunt Clair, Tommy Irene's mother. They lived in the bottom land, low land along the river, with Uncle Block and a table full of kids; they were all tough and fierce. Tommy was the middle child of two brothers ahead, a sister behind and a baby brother. That was a lot of stomachs to fill with such heedless ways as Block Collins lived. But, as WC's mother said, "They were lucky to have any kind of roof over their heads." Old Dedge complained about them—said they shamed him; didn't own a pot to pee in, and he was only married into the family. At any rate, when Mr. Bell dismissed the class, Tommy's only thought was to find WC, give him a piece of her mind, deliver the letter and tell him the news.

He was not hard to find. He was sitting on the steps of the school house, squeezing his knees to his chest, tucked up against the wall of the building as children descended past him.

"There you are. I thought, big chicken that you are, you would have run on home by now. Where you been?"

"Right here. Waiting."

"Waiting? For what?"

"I have to talk with Mr. Bell."

"He's smoking mad at you."

"Yeah, I suppose."

"I hate you. Pee on the seat!"

"I know. I'm sorry I did that."

She pulled at her butchered hair as she crossed the steps and leaned on the railing.

"It's ok . . ." She sat on the same step he was on and smiled secretly.

"Mr. Bell gave me a pan of water and soap and told me to wash up. You know where. Made a world of difference. I haven't itched since. Did you think teachers did that?"

"I don't know. Mr. Bell's nice though, and that's why I have to talk to him." He stood decisively.

"Hey," she protested, and stood herself. "I've got something important to tell you."

She slid a hand into her pocket and brought out a tightly folded sheet of paper. She waved it under his nose.

"I got this to give you, too. It's for Aunt Della."

She snatched it away just as he reached for it.

"Say, 'please.' Say, 'Pretty please.' "

"Dang it, Tommy Irene, I have to go. Meet me at Red Breaks when I get done."

"No, wait, I'll give it to you. It's real important. C'mon back, I have to get on home."

She followed him up to the landing.

"You go in there and Mr. Bell is going to give you hell fire."

He had entered the dark opening, hesitated to allow his eyes to adjust to the shadowed gloom of the room. Mr. Bell was at his desk, head down, pencil in hand, writing.

"Mr. Bell, sir?" he offered.

"Is that you, Warren Carl? Come on up."

WC walked the aisle, but stopped in the light flooding between the first row and the low platform that raised the teacher's desk above the classroom.

"Thomasina, I see you peeking at the door and do not believe your presence, as distant as it may be, will be required. Run along."

WC turned and saw her step into the door opening. She waved at them, smiling ever so toothily.

"Go on!" he waved her away. "Meet me at Red Breaks, like I told you."

"Bye, bye," she said, and turned and tromped down the stairs, abusing each step.

Mr. Bell dropped his pencil to the desk, teepeed his fingers under his chin and looked at WC.

"Where did you go this afternoon? I guessed you went home."

"No. I cleaned the outhouse seat and sat in the woods till school let out."

"You caused quite a commotion."

WC nodded and looked his teacher in the eye.

"Yes sir, I made you a mess, and if you intend to give me a whooping for it, you better do it now."

"Why would I want to do it 'now'?"

"The only reason I came to school today was to let you know I won't be coming back. It's my last day. I'm quitting."

Mr. Bell rumped his chair back, left his desk, and sat on the edge of the platform.

"Do not do something like that, Son. You have a good mind. The only reason you've not learned to read and write is all the school you've missed, being in the fields and woods so much. Never gave yourself a fitting chance. I know about your work, but stay, at least, until you get the reading and writing. Just a little more time."

"I'm sorry about the reading—how I could not remember from one time to the next all those sounds. But I never had to care about it. And I thank you for the help. But my quitting is not about work at home. I have other reasons."

"And I cannot imagine any of them important enough to steal away your education."

The boy's smooth brow frowned and he looked at the floor.

"Sorry, Warren. I don't know everything, do I?"

WC was silent and rooted.

"Is there anything else you want to tell me?"

He shook his head, no.

"Am I able to change your mind about this?"

WC looked up.

"No sir, I've settled myself on this. I just came to tell you, because--"

He hesitated, glanced away and scratched the back of his neck.

"Because—I thought you would care."

The man stood, slid his open coat aside, putting his hands in his pockets, and looked down at the boy. He nodded.

"I do not agree, Warren Carl, but I see your mind is made up and I will not say any more against it."

A school room resting from a day's activities can take on such hollowness. The sudden departure of such a large number of children and the resultant vacuum from sound and energy leaves the room to creak with its emptiness. It was that "clearing out" the teacher and student both felt now—the parting of ways and settling of accounts.

WC fixed on the man's shoes, until finally, he looked up and asked, "Are you wanting to give me a licking?"

Mr. Bell smiled.

"No. What you did was wrong and deserves one, but what would the point be now? You run along. No hand will raise against you here."

WC turned to leave, but turned back again.

"Mr. Bell?"

"You want to re-enroll?"

The boy almost smiled.

"No, but would you mind if we shook hands?"

"It would be my pleasure."

They took hands and WC pumped twice, then headed up the aisle.

Mr. Bell saw the boy's shoulders were not as straight as when he entered, and he followed him to the door and watched him go down the steps.

"If you change your mind, you come back and know you're welcome. You hear?"

WC waved and then tore off through the yard hollering.

"You're a good man, Mr. Bell. Almost as good a man as my—"

That was all the teacher could hear as the boy's voice was lost to the distance opening between them.

* * * * *

Tommy Irene was sitting on the edge of the gully the kids all called Red Breaks. She had worked off a clod of red clay from one of the ribs protruding from the eroded ridge and was snapping it into pieces and watching them tumble down into the ravine below.

"What did you have to talk to Mr. Bell about? Did he whip the daylights out of you? I was going to show him my rash you gave me, but he said it wasn't needed. What did you go back in there for?"

WC was just sitting down.

"Why don't you give your mouth a rest?"

"My mouth is doing just fine."

"Be quiet a minute, will you?"

"Here. You want this?" She gave him the remaining hunk of clay and broke another for herself.

He began throwing bits of it at a rock below them that had obviously already been pelleted. She crumbled hers into a fine dust into her lap. But she could stand only so much silence.

"I got to be going home," she warned. "Daddy will be mad."

WC knew Uncle Block was rough on Tommy; she paid for the least little thing she did. Once, he had seen him whip her to the ground with an empty burlap sack and wallop and wallop her about twenty times. He had accused her of spilling out his jar of moonshine, when it was really the two older boys, Bill Philip and James, who had drank it themselves and laid the blame on her.

"What does your old letter say?"

She brushed the dust off her pants, clapped her hands together and rubbed them on her rear as she knelt beside WC. She took the letter from her pocket and held it out to him.

"You got to give it to Aunt Della. But it says Uncle Otis and Aunt Ada are inviting all the family to their house again—for a family gathering. There's going to be a fish fry and we can listen to the radio. Uncle Otis will probably have his harmonica and we'll all sing."

WC took the letter and unwadded it.

"That's what it says? We're invited to Uncle Otis'?"

“Uh-huh.”

“I reckon we won’t be going.”

He refolded the letter and stuck it in a front pocket.

“Won’t be going? Why, in Sam Hill, wouldn’t you be going? Don’t you remember it was the best time? I sat on the porch swing between Aunt Clair and Aunt Ada eating and singing.”

“I remember.”

WC relaxed back and pillowed his head on his hands.

“I need to think. Let me be just a while.”

Tommy Irene copied his movements and laid back as well. She remained still a few moments and then restlessness overtook her. She pulled one leg up and crossed it with the other. That did not last long, and she kicked her legs out straight again. She rolled onto her stomach. She let spit drip into a crack in the dirt.

“Might get chiggers, laying here.”

WC said nothing; his only movement was to close his eyes and put a finger to his lips.

“Ever have chiggers?”

“Dang you, Tommy Irene! Can’t you ever shut up? Don’t you have any thoughts yourself? Yap, yap, yap. You’re worse than a cat with a mouse.”

She shot up from the ground to her knees.

“Hey! What did I do? What’s got you belly-aching?”

“Your big flooding mouth is what’s belly-aching me! Your ugly face! Your freckles, your teeth, your whole entire skin makes me sick.”

She threw herself on him, sitting on his stomach and pinning his wrists into the dirt. He bucked and twisted trying to throw her off, but she dug in and hung on. He poked his nails into her wrists and tried to bite her arms. She spit on him to make him stop. He spit back up.

WC finally twisted a hand free and pulled her onto her back. She kicked at him, but he fought through her churning feet and sat on her stomach, holding her down. By now, they were both too spent to fight any further—they simply panted and snarled at each other.

"I ought to pitch you into the gully," he threatened.

"Go ahead, see if I care."

WC rolled off. "Aw, shoot, I don't want to fight."

The children lay there, catching their breath.

Finally their panting subsided and WC sat up.

"You still want to know why I went back to talk to Mr. Bell?"

"Don't care if I do."

"I told him I quit. I wasn't coming back to school."

She sat up.

"What you want to quit for? Aunt Della tell you to?"

"No. She'll be against it."

"Well, why you quitting?"

"I have my reasons."

He picked up a lump of clay and hefted it.

"I'm sorry about what I said. I've been rotten to you all day. You better get on home. I don't want to be the blame for Uncle Block mistreating you."

"You wouldn't be to blame. I had to give you Ma's letter."

They both stood and started for the road.

"But will you go to Uncle Otis' for the party?"

"No, I don't believe we will."

She stopped and tilted her head to one side. "Why, for heaven's sakes, not?"

WC faced her. "Last time Ma and me went, old man Dedge said he wasn't letting us off the place again for such doings."

"Oh."

CHAPTER SIX

THE PIGS

Trouble waited for WC back at the house—a nagging, meddlesome caller with no manners. Old Trouble plunks down and says, "Here I am," without offering any apologies, and the only gift it brings is itself, rude and demanding. It doesn't show up at the back shed, either, where it can be ignored until it feels it's unwanted and leaves. No, trouble puts its feet under your table, challenging to be submitted to and slaved over, or thrown out—a confrontation from which your mind hardly ever rests.

WC's trouble would only become dangerous, as evidenced by his mother's burns this morning. His own resolve to resist old Dedge's insults and bullying was further indication it was time for him to leave home and take himself out of harm's way. Also, with him gone, he reasoned his mother would be safer, because it was WC the old man bullied and complained about. In this case, it might look like trouble had driven WC from his own house and had "won." But that was not how WC saw it. He was leaving trouble to itself: misery meet misery. How could anyone call that "winning?"

How do you do it, though? How do you just leave home? He was not one to run off in the dead of night, not tell anyone, and not have a direction to go. He needed more than an impulse to lead him away. He needed to take one step, do one thing, see how it turned out, and then decide what had to come next. All day he had tried to think what that step might be. It was certain he needed to tell his mother and be just as fair with her as he was with Mr. Bell. However, the only answer so far was too simple, without hope and plan, and one Della would not accept: "Ma, I can't live here any more. I'm leaving home."

She would have a fit: shout, pour tears, sling guilt—why, she might even try to whip him into submission. But it would not stop him. No matter what, he was determined to leave, committed to whatever might be seen as a first step.

He stopped at Brogan's Knoll (the newly named site of the recently deceased pair of shoes), where he paid abbreviated respects (spitting), retrieved the hidden shovel and ran the remaining distance home.

Della stood at the well and paid little attention to WC's approach. A line of bedding hung limp and near dry behind her. Half the washboard disappeared into the gray, slick water of the wash tub, which sat on a bulky table close to the well. She laid the washboard aside, dipped a metal pail into the tub, carried it to the four-o-clocks and moon flowers bordering the steps on the porch and carefully, slowly watered them, making sure the moisture was not wasted in run off.

Della had a passion for cultivating and nurturing plants of all kinds, and wherever flowers or shrubs could be managed and thought to brighten, she dug them into the ground. Her "pride and joy" roses grew on the morning-sun side of the house: some on trellises, some in a hedge row, and some amongst rocks set into the sloping ground. Clematis blooms nearly suffocated one of the porch posts every season. There were lilies, day-lilies, daisies and all manner of spring flowers around the house. There was not a week from summer through fall that something was not blooming.

She waved at WC as he entered the yard.

"Help me with the washtub."

They each took hold of a handle on one side and dumped the water over the edge of the table into a slab wood catch basin Sonny Lee had made for her. It flowed from there into a trough that channeled and spilled the water to her bed of dahlias and cosmos around the well.

"I'm pleased to see those brogans aren't anywhere around your feet. What happened to them?"

"They died. Dead and buried."

"Well, I haven't time to wonder on that."

"How are those burns?"

She held out her hands. The blisters had been pricked and drained with a hot needle.

"They're not so bad, as they look," she downplayed their effect.

WC winced at the sight of the loose white deadness.

She grabbed a handle of the tub.

"Let's put this away and then you need to help Custer."

"What's he doing?"

"He's fixing to slaughter pigs and butcher."

"Today? It'll cool tonight, but it won't cool enough to hold meat. Don't let him do it, Ma, it's a waste."

"He wants to sell pork and sweet potatoes in Little Rock."

"The heat will spoil it."

"It's not my responsibility. He has his mind made up for killing today, and that is all I know."

They hung the tub on a hook at the side of the house.

"Oh. Tommy Irene gave me this."

He dug the letter from his pocket and held it up to Della. "It's from Aunt Clair."

"Is that right?" She climbed the porch steps and settled herself on the rocker, prolonging the pleasure of news from her sister before she unfolded the paper and began reading, curling wayward hair around her finger.

WC leaned against the house looking over her shoulder. He heard her grunt. She even smiled.

“Does it say Uncle Otis is having a family gathering at his place?”

“Yes, but it also says your Uncle Louis from Detroit will be visiting the end of the month. That’s about three weeks. Otis and Ada are inviting all the family for the whole weekend to celebrate. Lord, the last time I saw my brother Louis, you were just a baby.”

“We going?”

She snapped her head around to look at him.

“Of course, we’re going. What makes you ask such a question?”

“Last time we went, old Dedge said we—”

“Wild horses couldn’t keep me from my family.” She stood putting the letter in her apron pocket.

“Run inside and get you some corn cakes I fried. Then see about helping Custer out back.”

He pushed off the wall, relieved she would not be hindered by the old man’s threats. Inside, at the table, he stirred a lump of butter into a saucer of sorghum. He daubed the flat, round, crispy cake into the thick syrup, bit half of it off and chewed it to the back of his mouth. He licked what was dripping from the remaining half. It was crunchy, deliciously sweet, and he was ravenous after giving up so much of his lunch to Tommy Irene. He swallowed, forcing down some of what was in his mouth. To free his hands to prepare another, he stuffed the rest of the cake into his mouth. His cheeks expanded to closely resemble the mumps. He could hardly chew. He could hardly breathe. His mother would not have been proud.

WC carried another cake out back and saw the boiling barrel sitting over hot coals. The pig would be dunked into its scalding water to loosen the hair. Dedge knelt at the fire, fed it and fanned smoke from his face. Steam rolled out the open end of the barrel. He took a bite of the cake, chewed it down and licked his sticky fingers before looking into the barrel. It was beginning to rumble.

"Took yer time getting home. Where are them shoes?"

"They up and died." He chewed exaggeratedly, making smacking sounds and zeroed in on Dedge's neck.

"They cost yer ma a pretty penny."

"Did not. They were used shoes."

Dedge stood and rocked unevenly.

"What do ya have to say from this morning?"

"I said everything there was to say."

The old man leaned closer. His words smeared together.

"Yer sure are one pestering wart to me."

His breath stepped WC away.

"You smell like whiskey. Ma told you not to do your drinking on the farm."

"'Ma told ya, Ma told ya,'" he sneered. "Well, the only 'Ma' I listen to lives right here."

He patted the area of his coat right over his heart.

WC heard something slosh from inside the coat.

The old man turned his back on WC and stretched his arms up to the heavens, beseeching the liquor gods.

"Why do I live like this? Shot up and crippled! Living poor, hand to mouth, in a house of spite, without what is owed to me. Well, by God, I'm a man. With a right to take a swig if I want. We don't let nobody's 'Ma' tell us what to do, do we, Ma."

He opened his coat and spoke to his inside pocket.

"Why, hello there. Dear, darling mother. How ya doing?"

Old Dedge withdrew a bottle and showed it to WC.

"Meet Ma. She says it's time to say hello."

He tipped the bottle and WC watched the old man's Adam's apple move up and down several times. Dedge corked the bottle as he wiped his lips on his sleeve.

"Well, ain't that a preacher's look on yer face. Want some?"

He pushed the bottle toward the boy.

"I wouldn't touch the hateful stuff." WC's appetite had fled, but he bit into the corn cake for bravado's sake.

"Yeah, and I wouldn't waste it on ya."

"I want to know why you're wanting to slaughter and chance having the meat rot."

"It won't rot. The weather's cooling tonight. And chew with yer mouth closed. Ya make me sick, watching."

"Don't watch." WC crammed all the cake in his mouth, rolled his eyes and hummed with pleasure.

The old man sneered and then tested the water with a finger.

"How we suppose to kill pigs, scald the hide, scrape the hair, and get them all butchered before night comes?"

"We ain't going to butcher them. We're slaughtering three or four little ones and leaving them whole. Some of them Little Rock 'lah-tee-dahs' will pay anything for suckling pig this time of year."

"I wonder what they'll pay, if they get a good whiff of them."

"I told ya, they ain't going to spoil so quick as tomorrow. So go in the pen and start bringing out the least ones, while I get the rifle."

Dedge tottered into the house. He heard the pigs squealing, as he lifted the single shot bolt action 22 rifle from its pegs over the door. He poured half a box of bullets into his hand and fumbled them into his side pocket. He slid the bolt back, loaded the chamber and locked the bolt back into position.

In the time it took him to cane himself to the back of the house, WC had already tied two pigs to a pen post and was tying up a third. All the animals protested shrilly.

"Them the smallest ones?" Dedge called out. He stood beside the crate he had placed thirty feet from where he intended to shoot the pigs.

"It's three of them."

"Where's the runt? I want to be rid of it?"

"I couldn't catch him. He's too fast."

"You get him next, after we finish with these. Feed the fire. I want the water scalding hot."

Dedge steadied himself down onto the crate and laid the rifle in his lap. He took a large jackknife and whetstone from his side coat pocket and began circling the blade against the stone, raising fine grains of sands as he cut a keen glint into edge.

WC laid split wood into the coals surrounding the base and sides of the slightly tilted barrel. Flames immediately ignited, ran up the wood and began to curl around the sides of the barrel. Moments later, the steel began throbbing.

Old Dedge pointed his knife at a bucket.

"Take some of that corn and lay a trail towards me. Turn that first pig loose and give him a handful to get started."

WC sifted a last meal through his fingers to each pig and dropped a few kernels in a line towards Dedge's crate. He left a good handful in a pile to hold the pig still. He untied it and joined Dedge at the crate.

"You want I should shoot? You know I have better aim."

"I don't know any such thing. Been pulling triggers most of my life."

"That doesn't change I'm steadier with my aim."

The pig began feeding on the loose kernels, and Dedge snapped the knife closed and slid it back in his pocket.

"Shut yer trap, boy."

"You have to get him between the eyes. You've been drinking. Let me do it; you'll make a mess of it."

Old Dedge swung the rifle around and poked the barrel against WC's chest.

"I told ya to shut yer mouth."

WC stepped back, rubbing the place he had been struck. His eyes were wide, astonished.

The old man stood and stepped closer, crowding the boy back toward the pig and the fire.

"I think I got yer attention. Yes, I believe yer hearing me better, now."

He raised the rifle to WC's head, cackled, and sighted in on the bridge of his nose.

"Yer thinking I have plenty of reason to pull this trigger—ain't ya? Well, boy, how's the seat of yer pants?"

WC looked toward the house.

"Call yer ma, why don't ya? Maybe she'll come and change ya." He laughed at himself.

"Here's what I want ya to do. Go back there and hold that pig still." He waved the rifle toward the line of kernels.

"You want me to do what?"

"Go and hold that pig!"

"You're crazy to think I'd ever do that."

Dedge grabbed WC's overalls and threw him stumbling and falling into the pig. He pulled the firing knob back and raised the stock up to his cheek.

WC looked up and saw the muzzle aimed at his face. He rolled to the side and heard the sharp sound of the rifle. The pig began squealing madly, struck in the snout. It rubbed the gushing wound against the ground, trying to wipe the pain away.

Dedge was reloading, but the clump of small bullets dropped from his hurried fingers.

WC rushed him and twisted the rifle from his hands, forcing him to his knees. He closed the bolt on a loaded bullet, snapped the knob back and aimed at the bawling, tortured animal. He waited, holding his breath, until the pitiful thing swung its head up, and then he fired. It dropped—its struggling ended.

He ejected the spent shell into the air, reloaded another, aimed, and shot the second pig where it stood by the pen. It fell without a sound. The third moved to finish the remaining kernels of its neighbor and was dropped in mid feast.

WC turned to the house and hollered.

"That's the last of the shooting, Ma. The pigs are all killed."

Dedge reached for his cane and stood up.

"Thought I was going to shoot ya, didn't ya? Maybe I was. Maybe I wanted to. Ya know I'd like to."

He pulled out the jackknife again, opened it, and started for the first pig.

"Maybe sometime I will. Sure did scare ya, didn't I."

The rifle suddenly felt heavy to WC and he switched hands and knelt down to gather all the loose bullets Dedge had spelt. His heart raced and he was short of breath. He felt dizziness entering his head, and he slumped onto the crate; the rifle across his knees. The bullets dropped out of his powerless hands.

Old Dedge began humming a tune, as he made a gutting cut into the pig he had turned four legs to the sky.

The scalding barrel drummed and WC laid his head on the rifle to still the rolling darkness there. But pulses dropped into his stomach and nothing could prevent the heaving. What was inside, turned out. He gagged and let go... He moaned and then did it again... He shuddered and spit; wiped tearing from his eyes.

"Scared the puke right out of ya, didn't I."

Dedge smiled back triumphantly from the gashed pig.

“That’s the fear of God, ya got now, boy. It’s a lesson in knowing yer betters.”

He began making a sound like a banjo.

‘Dink, dinky, dink, dinky, dink, dink—dink, dinky, dink, dink.”

WC fluttered an eye open to see the old man grinning and extending one of the pig’s entrails from its body, plucking it.

“Ya take yer punishment right pitiful. Yer a sorry sight, that’s for sure. Never saw faster work on a corn cake in all my life. Yer a show, boy, a pure show.” He went back to his slippery work.

WC sat up, wiped the sweat from his head, and felt an energy returning to his body. He cleaned two bullets on his pants, loaded one, and put the other between his teeth. Old Dedge’s back was swaying to the twanging tune he was humming. WC leveled the rifle’s sights at the skin above his coat collar.

“Old man. Hey, look here, Ol’ Dedge.”

Dedge looked back over his shoulder. His tune halted and the grin bled out its merriment. He sat back on his haunches, reaching out his bloody hands.

“Now, boy, ya put that ol’ rifle down.” He cuffed at it, as if he could knock it aside.

“I told you this morning you would pay a price anytime you hurt me. I warned you.”

He cocked the firing pin back and set the sights on Dedge’s neck.

“How about if I take that ol’ knobby muscle off your neck?”

"Don't be pointing that gun at someone. I was only fooling with ya, a while ago. Don't be stupid or crazy."

Old Dedge rose to his knees and reached for his cane.

"Why don't ya just lay that rifle down and let's finish these pigs and eat some supper. Ya don't want to pull that trigger."

Steam surged from the barrel behind him.

"C'mon, lay it down. Lay it down, son."

"I'm not your son!" WC yelled and shook the rifle at Dedge.

"Good God, boy! Be careful."

"I'm nothing to you. Nothing! You hear me?"

"Take yer aim off my face, ya thumb sucking crybaby. Take it off or pull the trigger. Either way, I'm going to stand up."

He pushed his cane into the dirt to raise himself.

WC fired.

Dedge shouted and fell sideways to the ground. He pulled himself to his hands and knees, groaned, and sat back glaring at the boy. The front of his coat was one dark stain.

WC already had the second bullet loaded into the rifle.

"Look what ya did."

Dedge held his cane toward WC.

"Look at it. Ya splintered the end off—ruined it. Yer crazy."

He pulled his coat open and took out the bottle.

"How's your Ma doing?" WC asked.

"The dang cork came unplugged. It's almost all drained out."

Dedge lifted it to his lips and swallowed.

"Hey old man, tell me about my betters, now. What should I know about the fear of God?"

Della came around the house.

"What's the shooting for? I heard the pigs were all killed."

She saw WC holding the rifle across his shoulders and Dedge kneeling in the dirt holding his stubbed cane.

Dedge managed to stand and began calling the wrath of God upon Della, WC and the farm, naming all of them something filthy. He made his way to the barn, hunching lower to the shortened cane. WC and Della followed him as far as the corner of the house and watched as he entered the cavernous double doors.

He led Tom out of the shadows, stood on the mounting box and took a long drink from the bottle. He cursed its emptiness, slung it against the barn wall, where it struck hard, ricocheted and knocked his hat off. He cussed the hat where it laid and flopped across Tom's back. They headed out—Dedge draped drunk on the horse's neck.

"I don't think he'll be coming back, Ma."

"Don't fool yourself. He'll be back."

CHAPTER SEVEN

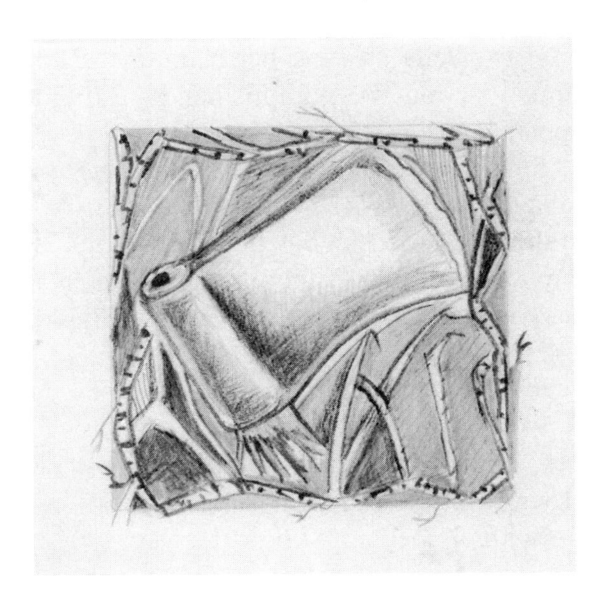

THE AX

All his life, it seemed, WC had done the work of a man, so it never occurred to him that he was not much over waist high to most men, skinny as one of their little fingers, and as likely to impress a potential employer as a frayed rope tied to a Brahma bull. But sooner or later, he would be offering himself, in all confidence, to a world that had little interest or hope in a runt that seemed all grizzle and no meat.

It was Old Dedge who provided WC the opportunity to take that "first step," make his first move from home.

Della had worried the old man would not return in time to take the slaughtered pigs into Little Rock to sell. She and WC stood looking at the splayed bodies outside the pig's sty, Della shaking her head, arms folded in condemnation, and WC with his hands resting loosely in his pockets.

"I know Custer when he's drinking; he won't be back today. My guess is he will be gone for two or three days at the least. We can butcher them, cure them and put them up for ourselves, but that is still such a waste of these young hogs. The profit was in selling them as suckling pigs."

"I can take them into the city. I can sell them."

"No you can't. Not alone."

"Yes, I can. I've been with Daddy lots of times when I was a little boy, and last year I went in on the tail gate with ol' Dedge. I know the way; I know what to do."

"Don't be silly."

"Look at those fields, Ma. I got them ready for harvest. And you want to tell me I'm silly, and can't drive a wagon to town, find a few people to buy a pig or two and drive home. C'mon, Ma, what do you think I am?"

He walked to the wood stacked by the barrel and laid split chunks on the coals.

"You know I can do it."

"I'm afraid for you."

"I know, but I would be all right."

She nudged one of the pigs with a toe.

"These should bring a good price. You shot them, didn't you?"

"Yes, I did." He stood beside her.

"What happened to Custer's cane?"

"It broke on something, didn't it?"

"Is that all I'm going to hear on the subject?"

"It's his cane. I don't have anything to say about it."

* * * * *

WC worked into the dark, dressing out the pigs. He quartered one and butchered it, expecting to sell it in pieces to those not willing to buy a whole pig. Della had earlier in the day set Gabriel in a pot to stew with carrots, onions and a chunk of butter. After she had taken the clothes off the line and made the beds, she rolled out dumpling dough, cut it into slices and slipped them into the rich, bubbling gravy for supper.

There was plenty of chicken left over. Neither Della nor WC would admit it, but they did not have the heart to eat that old bird. Both had filled up on the dumplings and gravy, sliced tomatoes, cucumbers, and corn bread. Gabriel may have flavored their meal, but technically did not become their meal.

Della had washed the dishes, stored the leftovers and sat on the porch rocker to rest. By the time WC finished drying the last dish and went to join her, she had her shoes kicked off and the neck buttons undone on her dress. She had dragged the chair closer to the edge so more of the heavens were visible to her past the porch roof. The sky was clear, bright, and her face was turned up to it.

"Feel like a long, tiring day to you, Ma?" WC asked, rattling his hands in his pockets.

"Yes, it does." She took a hold of his arm.

"Sit down. It looks like we have time to ourselves again."

He sat beside the rocker.

She rested one hand on his head and rubbed clumps of hair between her fingers. After a few contented moments, she raised the other hand out beyond the house.

"Moon and stars, moon and stars,
Reach out your hand
They aren't so far."

She spoke so privately, spontaneously, as if alone. WC had never heard the verse before and turned up to look at her. Her face was drenched in night light, softened and glowing, eyes jeweled by a starry surface.

Before he knew his mouth had opened he said, "You look pretty, Ma. "

"Lord!" she blurted back. "Do not. It is the darkness hiding all my faults."

She scratched her fingers in his hair. He could have purred.

"I never heard that poem about the 'moon and stars' before."

"They're just words I made up. But what if you could hold up your hand, and take some of the treasure out of the sky? If it poured into it? The treasure could be anything you wanted; you only had to name it... You want to try it, Son?"

He did not answer, but just gazed into her heaven.

"The sky looks like a trellis with silver, shining flowers blooming off it, doesn't it? I try to get something to pick me up, before I go to bed. You ought never to go to sleep without God giving you something for your weariness. Weariness wakes to weariness."

"Are you getting cold, Ma?"

"Yes, I am a mite, but I'm going to sit a while, yet."

WC went into the house and came back with a shawl he draped over her chest and arms. She settled into its warmth and smiled at him, as he sat on the steps below her.

"That's exactly what I mean when I say you wait for 'God to give you something.' Thanks, Son."

He was tempted to tell her about leaving home, but he was not about to tear down what the moon and stars were building up. There would be time for "telling" after his trip to Little Rock. There were many doors in that city to knock on and try to open. One of them had a job for him; all he had to do was find it and ask. With a job in hand, the news would be less painful to her.

"You know what the sky makes me think about?" he said. "I think about the river branch with all the trees along it, and a coon crossing over from the woods, rinsing off some old frog on the bank, eating it. In one of the deep holes, a big bass is waiting to suck in some crawdad scooting by. All that makes me think there are things you can see and things you can't see, but still you know they're there. And because you know what you can't see is there, it helps you to trust your own eyes more. You know what I mean, Ma?"

She nodded and grunted in agreement; leaned back, eyes closed, deep in contentment.

"You sound like your daddy."

"That's good. . . .Say the 'moon and stars' again."

She just smiled and slowly began rocking.

He waited, not wanting to force her peace.

"Moon and stars, moon and stars,
Reach out your hand
They aren't so far."

She opened her eyes and looked at her son.

"It's time I went to bed." She pinched her shoes together and waved at the sky. "Goodnight sister moon, good night, cousins." She pulled WC's ear. "Good night, little mister."

"I'm right behind you, Ma."

Della glided into the house.

WC unhooked the brass button on one of his straps and let his overalls drop around his knees. He stepped out of them and balled them up under an arm. He stood faded, in baggy underwear, on the edge of the porch with his hand held out like a cup. Not a pose to inspire any artist, maybe, but one, perhaps, to shake the celestial kingdom, as his lips moved silently, repeating his mother's poem. He finished saying something about a job being treasure enough. He closed his hand, not wanting to be greedy.

* * * * *

WC had been rocking in the wagon half the morning and had drowsed off several times. Dropping into potholes had shaken him awake. He had worn the coat Della had given him against the chill, and again, he recognized the gamble Dedge had made, slaughtering the pigs, had lead him to this opportunity. He would have to remember to thank the old man sometime; especially since he was right about how cool it was, and the meat would stay fresh today. He reached under the seat for something to eat.

Della had packed him a pail full of food for the trip. She had scurried around the kitchen in the light of the kerosene lamp, singing hymns. WC thought she must still have the madness of moonlight in her. She declared it had nothing to do with the moon, but the joy of living with Jesus.

She insisted it did not matter how much food was left in his pail, after he had sold the pigs he was to use some of the money to eat in a café and not be stingy with himself.

"Treat yourself good, now. Do just like your daddy would, if he were along. And make sure you get yourself a slice of pie. You hear me?"

"I'd like that."

"I mean it." She slammed the lunch pail down under the seat and swatted his behind as he climbed into the wagon.

"You need to grow some butt." She struck him one more time.

"Hey!" He said as he turned around, protectively, and smacked his fanny several times.

"I guess that's 'butt' enough."

"Do you think you'll make it home tonight?"

"No. Don't look for me before tomorrow, late afternoon or early evening."

Now, many miles from the house, he could smile as he snacked on a biscuit and several slices of the ham she had packed for the trip. Things were better without old Dedge: they could joke, talk easily. They could even dance.

WC heard blows and rhythmical buzzings from a distance, echoing, bouncing out from the heavy woods off to his left. He pulled Kate and Joe to a stop and listened. Joe rattled the wagon chains kicking against biting flies, but WC still was able to hear a snapping, popping sound, and then the limb-whipping fall of a tree. Even from the road, he felt the quake of it hit the ground. He heard a man's edgy shout.

"Now you finally got it down, clean it off before next week comes."

They were logging these woods.

"A job," WC thought.

Just that quick, here was the first place to knock on a door. He knew how to swing an ax and pull a saw.

Further up the road, he stopped the team beyond a group of newly built rough-sawed buildings: one livable as the windowless sleeping quarters for a group of men, another designated as an office, and the largest sporting a sign nailed over the door proclaiming, HASH HOUSE.

Timbers were stacked in a long, low pile. A team of four mules was backed to it, and the heavy wagon harnessed to them was already loaded, waiting to be hauled away. A man carrying a pad of papers stepped out of the doorway of the HASH HOUSE and flung coffee from his cup.

WC jumped from the wagon and walked through the field of weeds to the camp. He saw a discarded ax lying off to the side. The head was dulled and rusty; its handle had been shattered, and only splinters remained at its neck. He picked it up.

The man had moved out to a table, and a match was cupped to his cigarette. Smoke breezed away.

"Beg your pardon, sir, but could you tell me where I might find—"

"Kid!" The man blew smoke out his nose. "If you're looking for your daddy, he ain't here. No one's a daddy here, so get out, before you leave snot all over the place."

"I'm looking for the camp boss."

He turned away from WC, back toward the mess house.

"Lindsay," he hollered and watched the door. He dragged hard on the cigarette.

"That stupid son-of—"

"Mister?"

"Shut up, kid. I told you to get out of here." He brushed past WC and strode several steps toward the open door.

"Those logs ain't hauling themselves, Lindsay! You've burdened that bench long enough!" There was still no movement at the doorway. The man stuck the cigarette in his lips and cursed his way into the building.

WC heard a mighty growl, and then a pained yelp, just before something was overturned and thumped to the floor. A metallic, tinnish sound dashed against the wall. Suddenly the man appeared pulling the bull-stout driver of the wagon by his hair. He sent the bigger man galloping for the waiting team with a kick in his hind end.

The man walked back to the table, picked up his pad of papers and began looking through them.

"Mister."

"Get out of here."

"I'd say you were the camp boss, for sure."

WC dropped the ax head on the table.

"I found this in the weeds back there. Thought someone here might want it back."

The man glanced at the blunted piece of steel.

"Kid, that's a pile of bull droppings. Ain't any good to anyone."

"Would you mind if I keep it?"

"You better get out of here, before I make you eat that sorry wedge of steel with your rear end."

"Yes, sir, I'm going, but can I have it?"

"Are you weak-minded?" He looked down at WC for such signs, drawing in smoke. He dropped the remaining stub to the ground and drove it into the dirt with his toe of his boot.

"Take the darn thing with you. I don't care anything about it. I just want you gone."

"Thank you, sir." WC remained, however, switching the ax from hand to hand.

"You see, I found it walking up here to tell you I was looking for a job, and wondering if you might be interested in me?"

The man slapped the sheaf of papers against the boy's face. He held WC by the arm and began swatting him around the head and shoulders, all the while hollering at him.

"Give a squirt like you a job? A puny nut? What makes you think you could work here? This is a lumber camp."

None of it hurt. It was the indignity, the injustice that shocked WC. He would have preferred to have been dragged by his hair and kicked in the rear. That would have been man to man. But this humiliation with paper was disgraceful and took the strength out of his legs. They gave out, and he dropped at the end of the man's hand. It was so absurd he began laughing. The more the papers whipped at him, the sillier the whole thing felt and the harder he laughed.

Finally, the camp boss gave up and began gathering the papers that had fired out from his hand.

"Now, maybe you'll leave."

WC stood beside the kneeling man. He held out a sheet.

"Here's one you missed. I don't think I deserved any of that paper spanking, mister. All I did was ask about a paying job."

The boss snatched the paper and grabbed up the remaining ones.

"Go on, kid, get out of here."

"I still want to know if you have a job."

"If you don't want to be knocked silly, you better leave. Right now! Don't mistake I'm a man you can mess with."

"You're not so mean. I know mean and mean wouldn't have slapped me around with a wad of old papers. All I want to know is if I can work for you. I know how. I'm willing, but only for money."

"There isn't a job in this camp for a kid. We cut timber and haul it to Little Rock. That's work for a man."

"I've done such work, sir."

"Oh, yeah? Where? On your farm?"

"Yes, sir"

"Well—it's hardly the same. Look, I've got work to my eyeballs and don't have time to fool with you. If you're not satisfied with me telling you 'No,' go convince the owner to hire you. I wouldn't have any choice, then, would I?"

"Can I talk to him now?"

"That's a joke. You won't find Mr. Lester O'Dell on the job."

"Where would I find him?"

"Perched high up somewhere in Little Rock."

"Good. That's where I'm headed. Mr. Lester O'Dell." He marked the name into his memory.

"Just where might he be found?"

The man laughed.

"Ask anyone in the downtown area. But don't go telling folks I sent you. My best advice is to turn that team around and head back to dirt city."

WC nodded.

"Thanks for the ax, mister." He started for the wagon, but stopped and turned when the camp boss called to him.

"Hey, kid. You bring back a letter, now. Something with Mr. O'Dell's signature, saying he's hired you. If you do, I'll find trees with your name on them." He laughed, waving the boy on.

WC laddered up the wagon wheel and knelt in the bed, lifting tools out of a crate until he found a file. He spent the rest of the trip sharpening the cast off ax head, his lap layering in a gritty metal dust of filings. By the time the mules drew the wagon to the outskirts of Little Rock, the ax had an edge and was gleaming.

CHAPTER EIGHT

THE CITY

When someone has little regard for a big city, and comes to it without any appreciation, its sheer dimension can swamp a person and turn him back to its outskirts. Add to its size the marvels to be found and the frenzied activity of its galaxy of wondrous people, and the possibility of a big city's deluging effect to engulf and swallow the raw and tender becomes an even greater likelihood. However, when you think about it, it was just people who planned and put up the buildings. People hauled all the wood, baked all the bricks, laid the rails, strung the wires for lights—people like any one else. People lived here; people lived everywhere.

In Little Rock the railroad and river barge traffic helped keep the city bustling. Kate and Joe walked the wagon down the main street, along the trolley tracks, among the many other wagons and buggies and the few automobiles that then populated the city, and flitted in and out of the slower moving traffic. WC pulled the team to a halt. He had never been to this part of the city—to its heart, and could not imagine what all the buildings could possible hold, or what happened inside them. He gawked at the high rising buildings, attached one to the other, as far as he could see. The people, moving up and down the street, in and out of doors, looked eager and purposeful. Women wore strange dresses that packed extra finery at the rear; nets and feathers dominated their hats. Everyone wore shoes and all the men seemed to have a gold watch chain draped across their vests. There were side streets and alleys and behind these buildings were other buildings continuing the mystery of the big city. What, possibly, could all these people do? Would any of them want to buy fresh pig or know where a man named O'Dell lived? He held the reins loosely, his mouth agape.

"It's enough to take your breath away, isn't it?"

The deep voice startled WC and he saw a man standing beside the wagon dressed in a brown suit. He wore a gun belt below his black vest; a ribbon tie hung loosely from the collar of his white shirt. The man's smiling face was freshly shaved and graying blondish hair curled from beneath the brim of a derby. "The city. It's something to behold, isn't it."

"Yes, sir, it is. It would take some getting used to."

"Well, you have to move your wagon along or pull it over to the side of the street."

"I'll move on, but could you tell me where I might find a Mr. Lester O'Dell?

"Lester O'Dell?" The gentleman laughed. "You sure that's who you're looking for?"

"He owns the logging camp east of town."

"That isn't all he owns, son." He motioned for WC to drive the mules to the side.

"Where's your daddy?"

"I haven't got one. He died."

"Who came with you?"

"I came by myself. I'm selling hams and suckling pigs, fresh killed yesterday. Would you know anyone might want some? And I'm looking for work."

"You're not going to try to sell Mr. O'Dell some pigs are you?"

"No, sir. I have business with him though."

The man laughed and shook his head.

"Business with Mr. O'Dell, huh? All right, son, you promise not to shoot the man or rob him?"

"Mister! I'd never do such a thing."

"I didn't think so. See that big stone building back there on the corner to the left."

WC nodded. It was one of the tallest on the street.

"That's his place of business and I suspect he's in there somewhere."

He stepped away from the wagon, grinned and touched his hat.

"Good luck and you be careful."

WC took a loose grip on the reins.

"Are you the law, sir?"

"You bet I am, son. My name is Bill and you don't want to meet me again, now, do you?"

"No, sir."

"Don't be a bother to my citizens then."

"Not me, sir. Thank you for the help." As WC drove away, he turned back and waved timidly at the man who was following along the sidewalk.

* * * * *

WC had backed the wagon inside the wagon yard fence and attended to the feeding and watering of the mules. He dropped two hams into a burlap sack, slung it over his shoulder and set out to find Mr. O'Dell. The main street window displays astonished him: the richness and diversity of the clothing, the fineness of the furniture, the paintings and books, and whole stores with just shoes—amazing! He lingered longest fascinated by a washtub on legs with its own wringer. What that thing could do to a week's wash. He could only imagine.

Mr. O'Dell's building had windows big enough to drive a wagon through. WC nosed up to one and shaded his eyes against the sun's glare. The room was huge and open. Directly in front of him a group of desks behind a railing formed an "L" shape along the windows. On the wall to his left lines of people stood at a long counter, and men standing behind steel bars waited on them.

In front of where WC stood pressed against the window, a man at a desk conversed with a richly dressed couple sitting across from him. He noticed WC and motioned him away with jerks of his head.

WC remained, his eyes sweeping the unbelievable interior.

The man held a hand up interrupting his customer dressed in a blue striped suit. He set his pencil down, rose red-faced and glaring, and stepped toward the window motioning WC to scat. The wife beside the blue-suited man, sitting on the edge of her chair in a silk beige dress, watched the boy stand his ground. She raised an eyebrow.

"Shoo!" the man hissed. "Go away."

The woman raised the other eyebrow as WC stepped away calmly, lifted his chin high, and swung the sack over one shoulder.

It was not the welcome WC needed—doubt crept in. He inspected his reflection in the glass: bare-foot, dusty overalls exhausted of color, sagging at the seat, made droopier by the ax in his back pocket. What a sight, compared to what he saw on the sidewalks and in the stores.

He turned to the street, skeptical he was equal to all this. Nothing in this part of town was familiar or sure; everything was strange and bewildering. He did not know these people or their ways. He would walk in the door and they would throw him out before his footprints were cold. He considered leaving and trying elsewhere for a job.

He looked back down the street, the way he had just come, and thought, "I didn't walk all this way just to leave a few steps too soon. Am I supposed to fly away just because some fancy man in a suit flaps his arms at me?"

He really had not tried yet. Yes, he felt out-of-place, but how terrible to come this far only to lose nerve now.

"Best thing to do is step up and take your chances."

He walked to the entrance door but was stopped shortly after entering by a uniformed bank guard. The officer pulled WC aside and stooped to him, holding him by the collar of his shirt.

"What are you doing?"

WC was too frightened and astonished to answer.

The man tightened his grip, striking WC's chin as he did so, hurting and angering him.

"Ow! Let go—I didn't do anything."

"I said, 'What are you doing here?' " He gave WC a shake.

"Hey. I have business." WC dropped the sack and tried to pull the man's rough hand from his grip.

" 'Business?' Your business is outside." He turned the boy and shoved him toward the door.

WC stumbled awkwardly.

"Watch it, you!" He ran back, scooped up the hams and pointed his finger at the guard.

"You're in trouble now. Just wait."

"Keep walking—get out of here."

"You might as well start looking for another place to work."

"Is that right?"

"You don't look good in those clothes, anyways."

WC heard someone laugh off to the side and saw the woman who had been at the desk by the window. She watched the scene.

"Outside, you little clod." The officer grabbed WC by the back of his overalls, lifted him and began marching him out on his tiptoes.

"Mr. O'Dell won't like someone throwing me out of his store."

"You don't think so?"

"And Bill the Lawman—he might not shoot you with that gun he wears on his hip, but you had better hide when he hears you kept me from my business. That's who sent me to this very door."

The man halted and released WC.

"Wait a minute. How do you know the Chief?"

WC walked away. The guard pursued him out the door and blocked his path.

"Who are you?"

"I'm someone who thought he had business with Mr. Lester O'Dell, but I guess I don't."

"How could you have business with Mr. O'Dell?"

"That would be up to us, wouldn't it? But if you need to know what our business is, and he wants to share that with you, go and ask him. But for me, I'd just as soon keep it private. So I'll just go on back home and wait for him to come to me."

"No, wait. Let me straighten this out."

"Mister, I've been roughed up—treated like I was going to rob the place. I don't know if I want to chance any more of that."

"You'll be fine. I'll just find the right people and we'll see how we can help you." He motioned for WC to follow.

"All right." He reluctantly nodded.

They were blocked at the doorway by the same woman who had been watching them inside. Her husband now stood with her, his blue striped suit crisp and new looking. The tie he wore was tacked down with a golden pin. The woman's dress was bustled and shined a creamy tan. They were not arguing, but she was making herself perfectly clear about something, and the man was duly attentive. She glanced down at WC and smiled, but it did not in the least interrupt the flow of her discourse.

The guard walked WC near the end of the counter and was telling him to wait, while he found a supervisor. The woman approached them; her husband reluctantly behind.

"Excuse me, officer, but we would like to offer our assistance."

"Mrs. Shearcott."

"You seem to be in such precarious straits I thought that, perhaps, Edward and I should intervene and, hopefully, save the day."

The guard chuckled and shrugged.

"This little guy says he has business with Mr. O'Dell. He looks like he belongs in the barn, so I'm not sure what to do."

"Edward and I will take over."

WC combed his fingers through his hair and tried to mat a part on one side. The woman was very pretty, particularly with that kind of beauty one achieves if one can afford it. Yes, skin could look that soft, he thought, without the wrinkles of worry and weariness. Hair could curl and bounce like that, lips and cheeks can glow if you don't have to make your living on dirt. He was jealous for his mother.

The Husband stepped forward. He wore a look of irritation and concern.

"Why would you need to see Lester O'Dell?"

"I have business with him. Could you point him out to me? There's an anthill of people in here and we haven't met each other yet."

The woman laughed and said something about "a darling boy," as she moved beside the man.

The trolley clanged outside; WC dodged past the man and woman, excusing himself, to watch it rumble along the street. A young girl, half out a window, arms thrown to the wind, argued against her mother's efforts to bring her back inside.

"That looks like it would be quite a ride," he said to the couple who had followed him and now stood outside the entrance.

"But that straw hat must be nailed on that little girl's head, for it not to come off, don't you think?"

The woman was amused, but her husband was not.

"Young man, Mr. O'Dell is very busy and you have to have an appointment to see him. Do you have an appointment?"

WC had gone this far and if that was all it took to see Mr. O'Dell, he had one—whatever it was.

"Yes, sir, I got one of them 'apintmas.' Got two of them, as a matter of fact, inside this sack." He held it up as proof, hoping the bluff would be convincing enough to satisfy them.

The man shuffled his feet and huffed in exasperation, but his wife laid her hand on his arm.

"Take it easy, Ed. He's not one of your managers to bully."

"Yes, and he's not a stray puppy dog for you to pick up. For crying out loud, Alma, he cannot go in there and knock on Lester's door with a feed sack in his hand."

"Never worry. I will take care of it."

She took her husband's arm, walked him around WC and kissed him on the cheek.

"You get your hair cut and I will meet you at the dining room, after I take—" She turned back to WC.

"What is your name, young sir?"

"Warren Carl Thomas."

"After I take Master Thomas to see Lester."

"Don't do that to Lester. He'll never forgive you."

"I must have my curiosity satisfied as to what business this young man has with the great Mr. O'Dell. Just how will his self-importance stand up to the mysterious 'apintmas' this boy has poked up in that sack? It is all too delicious, Ed."

The husband smiled briefly, but then shook his head and held out his hands.

"You're lucky he likes you, otherwise, it would be your funeral. He would kill you for this."

"Well, he can do it Saturday night, because he and Louise are coming for your birthday dinner." She took WC's free hand.

"Warren Carl Thomas, get ready to meet Mr. O'Dell." She opened the door.

"Just what 'apintmas' do you have in that sack?"

"Fresh hams, ma'am."

"Ham? How very appropriate."

They entered the building. He followed along her hem, the rustling of her dress and the softness of her hand distracted him from feeling like a child in tow.

* * * * *

At every step, the woman's shoes clicked against the polished stone of the floor. Many heads turned and watched them. A few people nodded and spoke her name as she led him across the building to a set of doors. She pressed a button in the wall and WC worked his hand loose from hers.

"Fix your strap." She pushed the button again.

He pulled the strap up that had slipped off his shoulder and looked down at the carpet on which they stood. He dug his toes into it.

"It's like standing on a sweater."

She softly closed her eyes, nodded and smiled.

"I saw you struggling to make up your mind outside the window. You almost decided to leave and not come in."

"How did you know?"

"It was not so hard to discern."

He heard a noise behind the doors, as if something had dropped into place. One door slid open and WC was eye to eye with a uniformed boy behind still another door that looked like a steel cage. The boy pulled it open and the woman steered WC inside.

It was a small room that led nowhere. It certainly did not deserve such large doors, WC thought.

"Eighth floor, please, Richard."

"Eight. Yes, Madam." He pushed a lever and the room jerked upward.

WC grabbed the bars of the gate.

"The room moved!" He looked at the boy.

"Open the doors; let me out."

The boy looked away and sniffed.

The woman patted his shoulder.

"It is all right. This is an elevator—a machine. It moves from one floor to another, saving a person from walking up and down all those stairs.

It came to a stop and WC caught at his stomach. The doors opened and again WC was steered out and down a hall, around a corner to another open area.

The ceiling rose three floors overhead and massive wooden beams scrolled out from the four corners and met in the center. A chandelier was suspended from it; its crystal an echo of the expansive light freely pouring from the two window walls. The woman left WC and walked to a desk.

"Alma Shearcott to see Mr. O'Dell, please."

"Oh, Mrs. Shearcott, I'm afraid he already has his mortgaging officers waiting to begin a meeting." She stole a look toward the boy standing in the middle of the room.

"Oh, Rebecca, I am sorry." She tapped her head.

"I forget people are busy. I am too selfish, I suppose, to consider such a thing, when I came all this way to drop by for just a minute."

"Not at all. I'm sure he'd love to see you, if he—"

"Well, it would be just to say 'hello.' I would not stay long."

"Well, I—"

"Tell him who it is, dear." She smiled and then joined WC, who had not moved from where he had been left.

"Your name is Mrs. Shearcott?"

"Yes, it is."

"I'm pleased to meet you. And thank you for showing me where Mr. O'Dell is. I doubt I ever would have made it past that elevator."

"I doubt anything would have stopped you, but you are most welcome."

He was gazing at the chandelier. She contemplated his view of things.

"This is a lovely building, isn't it?"

"My Uncle Otis has a big house—a radio too." WC pointed at the chandelier.

"I've never seen such lights as those. You think that chain is made of gold?"

"No, I imagine it is brass."

"What about all those glass necklaces?"

"They are crystal and at certain times of the day they cast rainbows on the walls."

"I wonder who keeps it clean and shiny. Seems like a lot of work just for light."

"Mrs. Shearcott." The secretary held a huge door open and extended her hand toward the office within.

"Mr. O'Dell would be delighted to spend a moment with you."

"Thank you. Come along, Warren Carl."

Mr. O'Dell, a small man, strode from behind his desk, straightening his tailor-fitted suit coat and fluffing his silk scarf necktie. A heavy gold watch chain swung across his high buttoned vest.

"What a pleasure, Alma. Do you have time to sit a minute?"

"I know I am being a dreadful nuisance, taxing your hospitality, and Edward cautioned me against this visit, but Lester, I met this remarkable child outside your doors. He was determined to meet you and I am happy to be able to introduce the two of you." She turned and presented WC.

He did not hear one word of their conversation. He stood wide-eyed and open-mouthed, stunned with the feeling he ought to go back outside, wipe his feet and take a bath. The polished wooden floor glistened to a mirrored surface, and to his amazement there were no gaps between the joints. The throw rugs had the deepest, brightest colors he had ever seen and the desk was big enough to sleep all seven of Tommy Irene's family. Two wing chairs sat before it, gleaming in mahogany lustrous leather. Globes of light hung from the wood-paneled ceiling, and one entire wall, except for the counter and lower cabinets, was filled with gold lettered books. Paintings, some life size, hung in ornate gilt frames. Everything glimmered, nothing was out of place. WC blew air from his mouth and wondered what in the world he was doing there.

"Master Thomas?" Mr. O'Dell stood over him with a hand extended. WC saw a patient smile below the man's brushy moustache. It was trimmed, and a wax had given its graying blackness a matted, glossed appearance. Sideburns covered his cheeks, and the lengthy strands of dark hair combed over his head were not enough to hide the fact he was balding.

"I understand you've been looking for me. Mrs. Shearcott says we have business to conduct: that we have 'two apintmas?'" He shook his head questioningly.

WC wiped his hand down his pant leg and had his hand shaken in both of Mr. O'Dell's.

"Please, sit down."

Mr. O'Dell returned to his desk and WC scooted onto the slippery chair; his feet left the floor. He thought the man's face friendly enough and his voice seemed to smile and invite, but he was restless and in a hurry. He felt Mrs. Shearcott standing behind him: her hands rested on the wings of the chair. Mr. O'Dell cleared his throat, steepled his fingers and waited. WC knew he was expected to speak, but could not think of where to begin. He swung his feet trying to wind up a thought.

Finally, Mr. O'Dell laid his hands flat.

"Alma, if this were anyone else, I'm afraid I would be too pressed for time."

"You'll have my everlasting admiration, if you—"

"Might I have some water, sir, from your jug?" WC needed time to think.

"By all means." Mr. O'Dell poured water into one of the stemmed glasses arranged on a silver tray. He set it on a wooden coaster and passed it across the desk.

WC put it to his lips. He felt pressure mount behind his eyes as the man watched and waited for him to finish. He worried about slurping and worried about breaking such a silly glass made so thin a heavy breath would break it. He returned it to the desktop without accomplishing a clear thought. Mr. O'Dell immediately lifted it onto the coaster. WC turned and looked up at Mrs. Shearcott. She urged him on with a smile and motion with her head.

He took a stab at the first thing that came to his mind and reached into his back pocket and presented the ax head.

"I found this out by your logging camp on the east road." He placed it on the desk and Mr. O'Dell quickly moved a pad of paper under it.

"It was all rusted and blunted, but you can see I put it back in shape and it's better than new, now. Your boss let me have it. When I'm finished, it will be fitted with a hickory handle and have a razor's edge on it."

"That's commendable. Mighty fine work, Warren." Again he lifted his eyes to Mrs. Shearcott for relief.

"Really, this is quite an intrusion."

She leaned over the back of his chair.

"Is this all the business you have, Warren Carl?"

"No, ma'am."

"Well, you must get to the point. Mr. O'Dell is a busy, important man with many significant things to do." She sat in the matching chair beside WC's.

"Now, Alma, that's hardly fair, when I am holding up a meeting with Ethan and Russell."

"I drove Kate and Joe into town to sell fresh suckling pigs—that's how I came across your logging boss. I asked him for a paying job and he told me 'no.' But you're the owner, he said, and if you wrote a letter saying I was hired, he'd have to give me a job."

He paused a moment as he contemplated the palm of one hand.

"I don't think he put much faith in my finding you." Then he looked over at Alma.

"If it weren't for Mrs. Shearcott, I don't guess I would have."

"Lester, do not underestimate him or be fooled by his obvious humility. After what I saw him do to your poor guard downstairs, I have no doubt he would have tracked you down if you would have been on one of those Galapagos Islands."

WC smiled and looked questioningly at her. He wiggled to the edge of the chair, so his dangling feet touched the floor.

"And I believe your logging boss doubts my fitness for earning a wage. But that's because he doesn't know me. Mr. O'Dell, I've been knocking down trees since I could hold an ax. I've never shirked, or feared any work."

Alma interrupted, "What about your parents? Why are you not in school?"

"Daddy died three years ago. I never went to school much and, yesterday, I had to quit for good, because I'm going to live on my own—that's why I need a job."

"You are not old enough to live on your own."

"When you have to do something, ma'am, I guess how old you are doesn't matter."

She covered her mouth with a hand.

"Lester, can you imagine? He cannot be as old as my Eddie or your William, and not living at home."

"What about your mother? What does she think of all this?"

"Well, sir, she doesn't know, right now; I'll tell her when I get back home. She'll be hurt to hear it, but I hope to have work, so as to lighten the burden of the news."

"How will she get along?"

"She owns the house and has old Dedge she's married to. He'll likely do better, if I'm not there." He darkened and drooped when he mentioned Dedge's name.

Alma was curious.

"What do you mean 'he'll do better, if you're not there'?"

"Just that things will be better off. I can't say any more."

"Did that man abuse you?'

He frowned at her.

"I'm sorry. My greatest weakness is prying."

WC stood offering the sack, holding it over the desk.

"Mr. O'Dell, if you found a place for me in your logging camp, I'd like you to take these hams. No, I mean I want you to take them just for listening to me—for the time I took up."

Lester reached across and snatched the sack from WC before it was dropped on his desk.

"Let me set this on the library counter."

Alma walked WC to the window behind Lester's desk.

"You say you have pork to sell? How much do you have?"

"Two dressed suckling pigs and two front shoulders."

"I believe I could use all of it, if you would sell it to me."

"Not the shoulders. I want to give them to you, for all the trouble I've caused."

Lester joined them, clearing his throat.

"Now, Master Thomas, let's get a few things straight. I do not take payment for favors, nor is there a price for the discussion of business. Bribery is outside my moral system. I thank you, however, for the offer of your hams and its generous thought. I will not take them with the expectation of any obligation, but, I will buy those hams from you at a fair price."

He stepped back, hooking a thumb into his vest watch pocket and studied the boy before him.

"Tell you what," he finally said. "I will give you a letter directing Roy Stafford, my man at the camp you spoke of, to find you a job—at least give you a start."

Alma almost bowled Lester over, embracing him.

"You are incredible! Magnificent! I am so proud of you. I would never have thought to see this day."

"What kind of a man do you take me for?" He did not know what to do with his arms, so he patted her back—profusely.

"A stuffed shirt." She held him away, tightly in her hands. "A heartless, over-starched, stuffed shirt."

They laughed and she pulled him into another embrace.

WC was forgotten. He was left to try and understand everything Mr. O'Dell had said. The one thing he was certain of was that he was getting a job and it was going to say so in a letter.

"I do not want you bringing every sorrowful waif into my office, now."

"Oh, Lester, this is just the beginning." She drew away laughing and squeezing his arms.

She took WC's hand and started for the door, but stopped and stooped before him.

"Warren Carl Thomas, would you be so kind as to accept dinner with Mr. Shearcott and me at the hotel dining room?"

"I think not, ma'am. These are all the clothes I brought with me."

"They will do, except for shoes. No matter. We can buy a pair with what I will be paying for your 'apintmas.'"

"I don't know about shoes; I'm obligated to replace Gabriel, I accidentally killed yesterday."

Lester rounded the desk toward them.

"Killed? Who did you kill?"

"He killed Gabriel, but I am sure Heaven is just fine. Do not worry about it, Lester. Edward and I will look forward to Gabriel at dinner, and we will fill you in on all the ghastly details, later."

WC grinned. "Yeah, Ma and I looked forward to Gabriel at dinner too."

"I'll send your letter across to the dining room."

"Did you want the hams I brought?"

"Certainly, I want the hams."

WC was perplexed; he had not understood "bribery" and "moral systems," or "expectation of obligation."

"Should I give them to you, like I said, or did you mean to buy them?'

"The right thing for me to do is buy them, Warren. I'll send money with the letter. Do you trust me to send a fair amount? Would that be acceptable?"

"Oh, I trust you. Yes, sir."

He returned to the desk to retrieve the ax head and slid it his back pocket. He offered his hand to Mr. O'Dell.

"I can't follow everything that's happening so fast, but I want to thank you for the job, and tell you not to worry if I'll earn what you pay. I'll make you proud you wrote the letter—you'll not be sorry."

For all Lester O'Dell's fine clothes, for all his lavish furnishings, his mouth hung open; slack.

"Lester? Say something or close your mouth."

"Uh, yes. Yes, Warren, I'm sure you will." He put his hand in WC's and had it pumped twice.

Mrs. Shearcott and WC left the office. Lester watched the door close, then looked at his hand and wondered what had just happened to him.

CHAPTER NINE

THE LETTER

He lay in the bed of the wagon soothed in the bulky warmth of a quilt, the answered prayer on his mother's poem, and the memory of the fine taste of a slice of pecan pie. Shoes dangled, laces tied together, from the wagon seat above his head. Never had his feet been inside anything so strong, yet so soft you could hardly tell anything was on them at all. They were used, but fit perfectly, looked rarely worn at all. Mrs. Shearcott had given them to him along with a basket of hand-me-down clothes from her son Eddie. She had them delivered to the hotel. Most were too fancy and not meant for work. WC tried to turn them down, but she insisted. He liked all the underwear though. They came in two pieces.

* * * * *

At supper, Eddie did not appear to be very happy about the gifts. In fact, it seemed to WC, you could not have pleased him with a genie in a bottle. He complained about the food, about the waiter, about the smell coming from a certain place at the table; he even complained about being bored. Why his jaws were not slapped WC could not imagine. At one point, right at the hotel dining table, he went so far as to shame his parents, when he took a cigarette from his pocket and started to light it up. WC had snuck cigarettes before, but it was not something you flung in the face of your parents. Mr. Shearcott jerked Eddie from the table, and when they returned the complaining improved, but not his disposition.

Dessert ended before it started for Eddie, however, when WC finished telling his story about wringing Gabriel's neck and having him for dinner. Edward and Alma found it amusing, but Eddie, unfortunately for him, capped off an accumulation of sly insults directed at WC by wondering why he had to sit beside some "tiring, trashy, hillbilly."

WC did not hit him too hard. Certainly not as hard as was deserved, but hard enough to swell and redden his cheek immediately. He stood ready to take the bigger boy on, but all Eddie did was cry and hold the side of his face.

"Da-ad, he hit me."

His father sat with his arms crossed and smiled.

WC thought about running out, but sat back down to his pie.

"With the way you talk, I'm surprised you're not a fighter."

The boy bellowed.

"Edward, do something," Alma urged.

"He deserved it. It might do him some good."

"I mean everyone is looking."

Mr. Shearcott glanced at several of the nearby tables where forks were frozen halfway to diner's opened mouths. He waved greetings to their staring judgmental faces, and motioned for them to complete the utensil's journey.

Alma rolled her eyes.

"He's disturbing everyone's meal."

The father took his son's arm and led him from the table. Alma returned smiles from the neighboring patrons. WC sipped iced lemonade.

"My cousin Tommy Irene squalls like that. You would think she had her arm tore off."

Mrs. Shearcott reproached WC's "violent reaction," was critical whether it was really necessary, and said she was disappointed at his "swift employment of such crude justice."

WC shrugged.

She apologized for Eddie's rudeness.

"You should not consider what you've seen today as his usual behavior."

"He seems practiced at it, if you ask me."

Alma blushed. "I must confess to some excessive pampering. He is very intelligent, and I might add, quite sensitive in an artistic sort of way. But he has yet to attain your resourcefulness and self-sufficiency. How does one come by such qualities?"

How could he answer? He did not understand half the words she uttered. The letter from Mr. O'Dell had been placed next to his plate when the pie had been served, and since then he had been tempted by its presence. He moved it toward Mrs. Shearcott.

"Would you mind reading it, while I eat my piece of pie?"

"I was wondering when you were going to get around to the letter. You have a remarkable patience with something so demanding of attention. I am simply dying to know what it says." She tore the end of the envelope, puffed it open and took out a folded sheet of paper.

WC crunched the fork through the tip of the pie and lifted the separated piece to his mouth. Mrs. Shearcott was staring at him, her chin resting in her hand.

"Why did you not read this letter earlier?"

He chewed his bite of pie and looked away.

She leaned closer and whispered to him.

"Warren Carl, can you read?"

He thought about lying; he thought about not answering at all. But she did not deserve the disrespect of such a foolish pride. She deserved honesty and he deserved to stay honest—he was what he was. But he could not look at her when he answered.

"No, ma'am, I don't have my reading down."

He endured the brief lecture she gave on his innate talents and what he might do with a proper education. He was not all that attentive, nor did he blame her for the shame he felt. She did not understand. But it did spoil his first bite of pie—that he did hold against her.

He asked her to not tell anyone, as he was not proud of the fact. She promised and finally began reading the letter and the sweet flavor of the pie returned.

"Mr. Roy Stafford:

"This letter is to introduce one Warren Carl Thomas, who I understand you have already had the pleasure of meeting yourself. I have been persuaded by this lad to direct you to put him on the payroll at work and pay commensurate with his age. Keep him safe, away from injury, but make him useful and deserving of his wage. In your next report, I expect to hear something of my young protégé.

"Warren, please find enclosed a $3.00 payment for your fine looking hams. I believe it should more than cover the current price for choice pork. Here is to seeing your name on the payroll.

"Lester O'Dell"

Alma stopped reading, smiled to herself and looked out over the dining room. WC wondered how she could look so pleased and still be dabbing tears away from her eyes.

"There's more," she said finding a separate note in the envelope.

"My dear Alma:

"It is with good reason I suspect you are apprized of the contents of this envelope, and hope these arrangements with Warren meet with your approval, and that I shall never again fall victim to your greatest vice: doing good to others.

"I look forward to Ed's party and to the time I shall see you pay for every syllable in the description tossed my way—I believe you said, 'an over-starched stuffed shirt.'

"Mercifully yours for now,
"Lester"

"The man has a sense of humor. Why have I never witnessed it before? What a day of revelation."

She fanned herself and patted the hair around her hat. None of it was out of place, as far as WC could tell. He ate the last piece of pie and waited to see what would happen next—he had never sat at a table so long. Alma sipped from her wine glass and ran her tongue over her lips.

"I am so inspired about Edward's birthday party, now. We will roast your pigs and list them on the menu as ‘Apple Roasted Apintmas, Stuffed with Apricots and Scented with Thyme.’ I will make an ‘Ax head Rum Punch’ and we shall get absolutely tipsy from it.”

A man in a brown suit stood at their table and his deep voice complimented Alma on her choice of a dining partner. It was the Law. WC sat up straight and folded his hands on the edge of the table.

“My goodness, won’t you sit down for a coffee?” Alma took the man’s hand and motioned to an empty chair.

“No, I’m sorry, it can’t be done. I’m guest of His Honor; I expect to cost him a pretty penny for a steak.” He nodded to a corner table, where a man was spreading a napkin on his lap and studying the bill of fare.

“My, my, dinner with the mayor. I would expect you to be more discriminating of your company.”

“It’s a free meal—whether it’s appetizing or not.” He looked at WC.

“Mr. Barnston, my enchanting guest is Master Warren Carl Thomas. Warren Carl, meet our city’s esteemed chief law enforcement officer, Captain William Barnston.”

“How’s the pecan pie here, young man?”

“Mighty good, sir, but I have an aunt who makes better.”

Barnston covered his mouth and chuckled.

“Is that right? Where you from?”

“North, in White County, close to Beebe.”

“That’s Alvin Dedge country, isn’t it?”

WC laid his fork down and sat back.

“You know him?”

“Yes, sir. Ma and I share for him.”

Bill looked at Alma.

"Big man in those parts. His brother's a cuss and warmed a cell a couple of times for me. Alvin comes in and pays his fines. They're a pair." He turned back to WC.

"You're not driving back home tonight, are you?"

"No, sir."

"Where will you stay?"

Alma clasped her hands together and placed them on the table before her.

"I have every hope he will accept our hospitality."

WC frowned and scratched his head.

"You mean stay at your house?"

"Yes; you would have your own room."

"No, ma'am, I couldn't do that." He pushed his chair back.

"Oh, but you must. Would you deny us the pleasure?"

WC stood.

"I'm sorry, but I said, 'no.' I don't mean to be ungrateful for all you've done, but I'm not at ease thinking of lying in your bed."

"You plan on staying at the wagon yard, then?" the captain asked.

"Yes, sir."

"You tell Barney—he's the night man there—that I sent you down. Don't worry, Alma, I'll have one of the boys rotate past there every so often, to keep an eye on him."

"Thank you, Bill."

"Well, I'd better get back to his Honor or he might reconsider who is paying. Always a pleasure, Alma.

Warren, you're a sharpie. Stay out of trouble and don't be a stranger next time you come to town."

"Thank you, sir."

* * * * *

He swung the shoes into motion with a finger and watched them kick at the stars in the heaven over his head. He lay in the wagon guessing at reasons why he had resisted Alma's invitation to stay the night in her home. Something was not right. She was nice, mighty nice that was for sure, but she wanted to do too much—take too much. He had to set a boundary.

He felt the money in his pocket: three dollars from Mr. O' Dell and ten dollars from Mr. Shearcott for the two pigs and front shoulders. In the morning, he would buy breakfast and then go to the feed store for a rooster. He already had a name picked out—Michael. He had considered Bill and the name Lester, but the angel's name seemed more appropriate and traditional to his family. Before he dropped off to sleep, he remembered what his daddy had said the night they slept in Little Rock in this same wagon yard. "Don't stay up all night trying to blow out that street light."

* * * * *

WC continued to file on the ax head as he left the city, and was so absorbed in the work he was disappointed at how fast the mules got him to the logging camp. He climbed over the seat to check Michael, whose feet were tied together. The rooster glared over a wing at him and tried to peck his hand when he stroked its feathers. He took Mr. O' Dell's letter from the basket of clothes, put the ax in his back pocket and jumped down.

The only person in camp was Cookie, the cook. He told WC the camp boss was in the woods.

"Who knows when he'll be back? Wait if ya like, but keep to yourself. I don't want to bother with ya."

WC sat on the log pile and studied the progress on the ax. The edge was sharp and the steel behind it was feathering thin to take a deep bite and have little resistance when meeting wood. The tail, however, he would keep thick and flared. That would give the head weight and drive.

The boss was kicking at weeds and muttering to himself when he came out of the woods. He took his hat off and threw it to the ground when he saw WC stand up and approach him.

"Not you again! Turn around and clear out."

WC held out the envelope and kept coming.

"If your name is Roy Stafford, I have this letter for you."

"What's that? Let me see it."

"Mr. O' Dell sent it with me."

"Mr. O'Dell?" He turned a circle, cried for Jesus and almost slapped WC with his hat. Instead, he grabbed the envelope.

"You went and saw Mr. O' Dell?"

"You told me I should."

"It's already been opened."

"That's because it was sent to me first. You'll see when you read it."

Roy mumbled through the letter, stopped and reread it.

"He can't be serious. Hire a boy at a logging operation?" He strode away calling for Jesus again. Then he found Alma's note she had mistakenly left in the envelope.

"That's not for you. It belongs to someone else and you shouldn't be reading it."

Roy continued to read even as WC attempted to grab it away. He laughed when he read the words at the end.

" 'An over starched stuffed shirt.' Who's Alma?" He waved the note at WC.

"I wouldn't tell you"

He read from the note. " 'Ed's birthday party.' Alma and Ed? Is that the Shearcott's?"

WC folded his arms and would not answer.

Roy read the note again, lipping the words 'greatest vice: doing good to others.'

"Oh, I get it, now. You're some charity case for that Shearcott woman."

"Like hell I am," WC stomped for the wagon.

"Wait, kid, come back here."

"I ain't no 'charity' case for anybody."

Roy chased after him, through the whipping grass and turned him around.

"What are you so mad about? Come on back. You know I have to give you a job."

"You made me swear." He slung Roy's hand from his shoulder.

"And if that letter says I'm charity, it's a liar."

"It didn't say anything like that—I did."

"Then you're a liar."

WC kicked Roy's shins. When the man yowled and bent to sooth the pained area, WC blocked him to the ground. He dove at him, trying to slug his way through the man's screening hands. Roy rolled away and stood.

"Slow down, boy. I don't want to hurt you."

WC lunged to tackle him, but he was easily tossed aside. He charged again and this time was picked up in Roy's arms and lifted to his shoulder. His arms and legs were pinned so tightly to the big man's body he was unable to move them.

"Are you going to calm down?"

WC tried to wiggle and kick free. Roy squeezed him tighter.

"You've got too much pride, boy."

"I reckon I got just enough."

With nothing left to fight with, WC went to the weapon of last resource—he bit the logging boss. He was immediately dropped to the ground.

Roy pulled his shirt back to examine his shoulder.

"I can't believe you bit me, you little bulldog. I'm your boss and I'll fire you if you don't behave."

"I ain't working for you."

"You are too. Mr. O' Dell expects it. If you want to draw your first wage, you'll forget what I said. I didn't mean anything by that remark."

"Sure sounded to me like you did."

"Well, I shouldn't have let it out, but how did I know—I'm the boss and I say what I want. You going to fight every time I tell you something?"

"Over some things, yes."

Roy rubbed his shoulder.

"Wish I would have known what they were before. I mean, can you take orders?"

"As good as the next man."

"Man. Uh huh, Okay." He pointed back to the camp.

"Let's go talk and see what we can find for you to do."

They both sat on nail kegs at the work table and WC dropped the ax head in front of Roy.

"You remember this 'old pile of bull droppings?' "

"Don't tell me this is that ax you took out of here the other day?"

"That's it, all right."

"You do this on a grinder?"

"No, sir." He tossed the file on the table.

"That would take forever."

"Into Little Rock and back."

"You for sure do this yourself?"

WC nodded.

"This is good, kid, really good."

"When I finish the edge, you'll be able to soap your face and shave with it."

"I believe you." He studied the work.

"Could you do this with a grinder?"

"A lot faster than with a file."

"Have you ever worked with saw blades? Two man cross-cuts?"

"It couldn't be much different than a cradle saw for stove wood."

"What else you good at?"

WC screwed up his face and shrugged.

"I don't know. Farming things—working with mules."

"All you kids out here farm. What makes you any different? Why should I put you to work?"

WC tightened his hands into fists.

"Because I got lucky. I got lucky, because I went to the trouble of getting lucky. I walked into Mr. O' Dell's office—it scared me half to death—and told the man I was fit for a job."

Roy rested his chin in the palm of his hand and stared at the boy before him.

"You make a point there, kid."

"Mr. Stafford, I don't know what I'll be good at, till I do it. But I can tell you I'm no stranger to trees. I can knock them down and make them fall on a toad, if I have to. And I know hunting. It's something I never fail at."

"You're a little skinny to take trees down fast enough for our operation, but we'll find use for your other skills as we find them. Sound okay to you?"

WC nodded.

"What do people call you?"

"Most everyone calls me WC."

"All right. Be back here by daylight Monday morning, WC. Bring your necessities and your gun. We've got squirrels and rabbits in these woods going to waste. We'd all like to see Cookie expand the menu with some fresh game." He stood and walked around the table to WC.

"You'll work daylight to dark, just like everyone else, except on the Lord's Day. I'll put you on half wages to start. We'll see how you do."

"You'll see me do fine." He slid the ax in his pocket.

"The men here are barky rough, kid, so I want you to watch yourself. They are more than likely to treat you like they do each other."

"I wouldn't want it any different."

"Well, we'll see how long that lasts. Just stay out of their way and come and see me if they get to twisting your tail too much. You have a paying job and welcome."

"I'll be here Monday morning."

WC set the mules on a walk towards home and bent mechanically to filing the ax. His thoughts, however, were rehearsals—telling his mother what was now firmly in his mind.

Roy watched from the door of the HASH HOUSE. Cookie stood beside him, dragging beans into his mouth over the edge of his tin plate. He chewed and listened as Roy described, almost with a father's pride, the letter, the sharpened ax and the audacity of the kid he had put on the payroll. To prove it all, he showed the nasty bite mark on his shoulder.

CHAPTER TEN

THE TABLE

When you have explored and prevailed in an alien land, found unimagined wonders and riches and received honors, you have every right to expect a triumphant return home. Bearing an accumulated fortune and heroic with amassed new found knowledge, the adventurer can be excused for having "princely treatment" in mind—not everyone has taken that journey, seen the sun on the other side of the world.

WC's mother was at the porch steps waving when he drove into the yard. She followed him to the barn and smothered him in a hug after he jumped from the back of the wagon.

"Where in the world did you get those shoes?"

"There's a lot to tell. Is old Dedge back?"

"No, and it being Friday, I don't expect we'll see him for a while."

He handed her the money, pulled the basket of clothes to the edge, so she could see, and repeated there was quite a story to tell: about a man and woman who bought the pigs, took him to supper, gave him the basket of clothes and pair of shoes, and then another man who owned a whole store and bought the hams.

Before continuing, he told her to count the money.

"My Lord, you brought back eleven dollars."

"And I have some change money in my pocket." He rattled the coins. "I guess I did pretty good."

"That's more than we expected."

"I want you to see this, too."

Della followed him to the front of the wagon where he climbed half way up the wheel, reached to the seat and took the ax down and showed it to her.

"I found this at a logging camp. The boss there let me have it, because it looked worthless. You can see I brought it back to life."

"What were you doing there?"

"I asked him if I could get a job."

"You did not." Her eyes widened, imagining her little boy asking some brutish foreman for a job.

"He wouldn't hire me on the spot, but sent me to see the owner in Little Rock. It was the man who owned the store and bought my hams. We talked in his office on the eighth floor and he's taking me on—wrote a letter and everything. I'll start work on Monday, and have to leave home and live there."

It took a moment for the meaning of his words to reach her; he was so direct and decided. It was short lived, however, as she crumbled the money.

"You'll leave over my dead body."

She shook the bills in his face. It was ridiculous for him to think he was separating his life from hers—he barely stood to the top of her apron.

"No, you're not! Noooo, oh. Uh, uh. No son of mine is walking out like some ol' drunk clutching his bottle? Don't pout at me. I don't want to see it." She turned from him, flailing her arms.

"I won't stand by and allow you to rush your life away. Every time I turn around, here you come, less boy, less boy. I've stood by and watched everything stolen from you, until nothing is left but a plateful of hate to fill up on. And who knows how that'll turn out. Well, this is the end of it—I'm stopping it right now."

She paced between WC and the mules scolding him. She called blame on herself, and prayed heatedly. WC dared no answer—could not, as her voice rose, accelerated, and dominated. She threw the money into the air and smacked at the bills as they fluttered to the ground. Spit formed at the corners of her mouth. WC worried she would hurt herself. He had never seen her so angry.

Michael fussed and flopped at the rear of the wagon. WC released the young rooster's legs from the twine.

"Don't turn your back to me, young man; I'll slap your face right out of White County."

WC watched Michael pop upright and strut to the edge of the wagon. The rooster jumped to the ground, ran to the pig pen, flapped to the top rail and crowed. The lounging hogs all lifted their heads, turned to the new, but familiar sound, before returning to their prints in the mud. It struck WC as the surest of signs the animal was taking possession of his new life.

"Hey, you pay attention to me." She lifted his chin to force his eyes to her face. "You think I want my son working with a bunch of men who live foul, talk foul, and spread their filth to make every innocent wallow with them? I'm all there is standing between you and the devil finishing the work he's started with stinginess and hate. I'm your light to God, your plenty, your possibility, and victory."

He wanted to answer, take some credit for himself, give some to God, but he would not contradict her. Instead, he worked wordlessly, letting the silence answer she could not change a thing: unharnessing Joe and Kate meant she could not stop him; leading them into the barn declared she had lost whatever hold a mother held over a boy. His silence, his actions made it clear—there was no boy.

That truth, however, did not arrest her sense of authority and she persisted in trying to hold on.

"And if you think I care about a pocket full of money and a basket full of clothes, you've got the wrong mother. Get up to the porch right now. Sit down, while I straighten you out." She swatted his behind.

WC's face reddened and he turned and faced her.

"Don't hit me, Ma."

She turned him around and swatted him twice more.

"Don't tell me not to hit you. I'll hit you, if you need it. Go on to the porch and mind me."

He shook loose from her and stood his ground, daring more punishment. Nothing happened, however, except a shuddering of her breath. He turned to see her running toward the river branch, hiding her face in her hands. He called and chased after her, but she waved him away. Her misery choked into his throat and his eyes began to sting and wet. He fisted them before they could puddle.

He ran to the porch to watch the path she took into the wood line along the river. He sat in the rocker waiting for her to return, but thirty minutes went by and there was still no sign of her.

He pulled the screen door open and smelled supper. It was all but on the table. Fried sliced ham was kept warm at the back of the stove, coffee scented red-eye gravy barely bubbled in the skillet; a layer of amber grease skimmed the surface. Turnip greens and a limp rind of bacon stewed under a lidded pot, their bitter aroma puffed out occasionally. A skillet of crusty, fresh corn bread was turned out under a dish cloth. The table was set for two with freshly cut geraniums and pink roses arranged at the center of the table. The scene was so welcoming and natural.

He had lived these aromas and sights so many times; they were as familiar as his right hand—needed, but unnoticed. Today, however, with thoughts that he would never belong to this home again, its smells and tastes were inescapable, richer. They were filled with his mother and she invaded him, opened up spaces he had closed. He sank into a chair and laid his face on the table, unable to hold his head up. He closed his eyes against it all.

He would never submit to being enclosed and rocked while recovering from the high tension of spite or healing some wound of loss. No, that would never happen. But here, at this molting time, he held nothing back.

Alone, everything vulnerable came flowing out, streaming over his cheek and puddling to the table. In silence he surrendered all that was green and unripened. It stained into the coarse wood of the table. Agony came in waves, each time with fresh cries of losing his daddy, the life he wanted for his mother, and the resentment for old Dedge.

He could count the times he had cried on one hand. Now he had almost equaled all of that in the space of three days. He felt a fatigue he had never known. A fly landed on his chin and moved to the corner of his mouth, but he was unable to lift his hand and brush it away. A chunk of stove wood popped and hissed out a pocket of steam.

He opened his eyes, sat up and wiped them on his shoulders.

The cast off skin of his boyhood stained a dark spot at his place on the table. He was out of its reach now —tougher and safer. There would be no more tears; nothing would ever make him do that again. He was finished.

He stuffed his few clothes into a sack, along with two boxes of 22 cartridges, and set it by the door. He was leaving—with or without a blessing.

He did the evening chores with half an eye watching for his mother's appearance. He poked up the stove fire and added wood. Still she had not returned and it would be dark soon. The rifle did not need it, but he cleaned it anyway and placed it back over the door. He sat on the steps, sharpened kitchen knives and watched for her. Each flit of a bird drew his eye, every wind-blown weed turned his head. He was worried. The light left the sky and shadows spread out into darkness. The trees in the distance were lost in a black gloom.

WC lit a lantern and carried it down the path she had taken to the river. He listened for any sound of her, but there was nothing. He followed along the river to the bend, where it turned into the deeper woods, and called.

"Ma?"

But she would not have gone in there. She did not like the deep woods—they frightened her. He backtracked and searched the other direction, calling out for her, all the way to the foot of Hickory Hill. He climbed the rise, shining the light on the meadow and then walked through the cemetery. There was no sign of her. He returned home, hoping he had missed her. But the house and all the outbuildings were desolate.

She was just angry, he had thought, and needed time to accept what could not be changed. But now he feared she might be lost or injured and need his help.

WC gathered every lamp they owned and filled them. He set the first one at the beginning of the drive up and spaced the rest of them right up to the porch. Seven lamps flickered a warm path to the house and every candle he could find glowed around the rocker. He went inside and sat at the table, letting hospitality tempt her home. Once, he looked through the screen door to check on the lanterns.

It was not long before her step groaned on the porch and he rose with relief. He saw her through the door holding two extinguished lanterns. She set them down and began picking up the candles, blowing them out.

"The porch looks like a party. Think I might attend?"

He opened the door for her and saw that the other lamps were all dark and sitting on the edge of the porch.

"Where you been?" He asked disapprovingly as she walked past him.

"I've been with myself. And that's no way to speak to me. I'm still your mother and going to be your mother, until the Lord sees fit to carry me away. Come here and take these." She dumped the candles into his hands.

"Put those where you got them." She mussed his hair and went to her bedroom and closed the door. He heard drawers slide open and close.

"I went looking for you," he called toward the door. He slid the gravy and greens to hotter spots of the stove.

"I know. I saw your light winking in and out of the trees."

He waited, but that was all she said. The gravy came to life and he gave it a stir.

"Where were you?"

"At school."

"You went to the school house?"

"No."

She came out of the room carrying an arm load of Dedge's clothes and deposited them on the seat of the rocker.

"I went to the Lord's school—been truant too long. But now I'm hungry."

She joined him at the stove, but he turned her away.

"No, let me get a plate for you tonight." He pulled out her chair and she sat at the table.

WC carried the ham plate to her and forked out a slice.

"Thank you, but would you serve me another. I believe the whole hog wouldn't be safe around me tonight." He jabbed another slice and shook it to her plate.

"I ate at a fancy hotel dining room." He draped a folded dish towel over his arm and carried the pot of greens to her.

"Madam's vegetable?"

"Yes, if you don't mind."

He spooned her saucer full, laid the towel across her lap and bowed.

"My, my. I hope I'm dressed properly?" She placed her hand modestly at her neck.

"The prettiest woman here."

He cut the corn bread into six triangles, knifed under one and balanced it to her plate. He rushed back to the stove and poured the gravy into a bowl.

"And this, Madam, may look like gravy, but it's not—it's sauce."

"Oh, well then on the meat, please." She swept her hand toward his chair.

"Would the young man be free to join me?"

"I was hoping you would ask." He hurried his plate together and started a pot of coffee to boil.

"Now would there be any adventures you might like to share about your most recent journey? Like how you came to have so much money, fancy clothes, and shoes. Is the law, perhaps, running dogs on your trail this very minute?"

Talking had never been something he enjoyed. He had little passion for it. But now, he had such a story to tell he became electric, telling her everything that happened in expansive detail—even about Eddie's lack of manners and the gun belt around Bill Barnston's waist. He talked and talked, while she cut small pieces of ham, chewed them and emitted an occasional "Uh, huh," as her only contribution. Other times she would set her fork down, rest back into the chair and press her lips with the end of the towel. It reminded him of Mrs. Shearcott. He had picked up his knife and fork, but they had not cut nor brought anything to his mouth. They were instruments of gesture: the trundling of the trolley, the rising of the elevator, the spiral of the chandelier and the good crack on Eddie's cheek. He never advanced to eating. But it did not matter, for his hunger was to talk.

Her plate and saucer were finally empty and WC set them in the wash pan. He sprinkled cold water into the coffee pot to settle the grounds and then baby-stepped a brimming cup to her and sat down to rearrange the food on his plate. Della folded the dishtowel and set it beside her plate.

"When you leaving?"

"Monday morning, before daylight. I'll come back to see you after dark on Saturday."

She stirred sugar into her cup. The sound seemed to have an intentional musical quality and WC looked at her. But her eyes were unfocused, dreamy, fixed on the flowers at the center of the table. She raised the cup to her lips. It shook ever so slightly. She blew across its edge, sipped and set it, rattling, back on the saucer.

"You're all I've got of love in the world."

WC stood, picked up his plate to leave, unwilling to listen to any argument meant to soften his will. Della reached out for him.

"Stay with me. I'm not trying to hold you back. Sit down and let me tell you my story, or don't you really care about the journey I took today?"

She released his arm, gazed at her cup, bestowing full freedom on his decision.

"I'm not changing my mind."

"I know. That's not what I'm asking. I want you to sit down and listen to me. There's things I want to say."

She caressed the cup and stroked the fragile handle with the tip of her finger.

"I'm awfully attached, Son—it has to be said before you leave. I don't want to hold it inside and regret you never hearing it."

He looked at her, then set his plate on the warming shelf of the stove and came back and sat down. Silence eddied at the table for several minutes. She spoke again—softly.

"At first, when I went down to the river, I was hurt and mad—thought you selfish and spiteful, infected by Custer's ways. 'Go on, run off, boy, and try being a man and see how you like it,' I said to myself. 'You'll be back before you work up a sweat.' I doubted you. I was afraid for you and prayed the Lord to provide me the way to convince you to stay.

"And, oh, WC, I needed an angel. I needed that shocking goodness. But you know what I was sent? You know what the Good Lord had the nerve to send me instead?" She reached out and clutched his arm. WC shook his head.

"A snake! A cottonmouth came wriggling out of that river not three feet from where I stood."

She held herself and shivered.

"I swear I hate those things. I backed away and looked for a stick to kill it, like you and your daddy told me to do, but when it coiled and showed its mouth, I ran. I ran out of the woods, through the meadow and into the hills across from the cemetery. And that's where I sat most of the time, studying. . . .

"I came to realize there's more to you than 'running away.' It's where I knew my doubts and fears for you had more to do with doubts and fears I had for myself."

Della sipped from her cup again and rested the rim against her lips as she focused on the saucer below.

"I wanted to keep you. I wanted to keep something... But you don't belong to me. And you'll be all right—it's your time. It just came sooner than it does for most boys, and that's where I feel cheated...

"You're the most grown up child, I believe, there ever was."

A lump came to his throat, so he quickly rose and brought the coffee pot back to refill her cup. She set it in the saucer for him to pour. As she spoke, he dug a spoonful of sugar for her.

"It has worried me that the only lessons you would carry in life would be the ones you could blame on a goatish old tyrant and his meanness. Don't let me down, Son; be more than that."

WC nodded and licked the coffee-wet spoon dry.

"Don't worry, Ma. It wouldn't take much."

She chuckled and told him he was terrible. He agreed.

"One last thing," she said, as she pulled a short pale green stem from a button hole in her dress and held it out to WC.

"I picked this dandelion out there today; its head all puffed and aglow. It was silly, but I blew on it to make a wish, like when I was a little girl. All but one of the seeds floated off. Just that one was left attached there. I carried it around all the time I was walking. The seed is still there. It's a fussy little thing, stubborn, that will hang on forever, don't you think?"

WC held it up close to his eyes.

"I love you, Son. Love you."

She expected a response, but he was silent. It was too much to hope.

"When you go, I want you to remember who gave you that seed and how it was fastened and couldn't be shaken loose."

She drank more coffee, steadier now, as WC continued to study the small white knob between his fingers and the single brown seed rooted there. He spun it between his thumb and finger as he spoke.

"You never know where the other seeds are going to be carried and take root, do you?"

"No, they're at the mercy of the wind."

"Well, I know where this one is going to be from now on. Could I have one of those dollars?"

She pulled a bill from her apron and gave it to him. He laid the stem on the bill, folded the dollar in half, in half again and then rolled in into a tube and secured it with a short wrapping and tie of string. Della watched him unsnap the breast pocket of his overalls and nest the little treasure to the bottom before resnapping the button and patting the area protectively.

"I believe I'll always know where it is."

His mother smiled at him.

"I could enjoy another cup. Don't you want one?" She pushed back her chair.

"No, I'll get it." After he poured a cup for each of them, he continued to stand at the table, holding the pot.

"I make old Dedge mad and can't help myself anymore. He'll have less cause to be mean, if I'm gone."

"You're not to blame for what he does. He had already made his way of life long before."

She went to the rocker and gobbled together Dedge's clothes piled there.

"What are you doing?'

"It's something else I learned today."

She dropped everything in a heap beside WC's sleeping nook.

"There will be an empty room when you leave. Custer will fill it as soon as you're gone."

CHAPTER ELEVEN

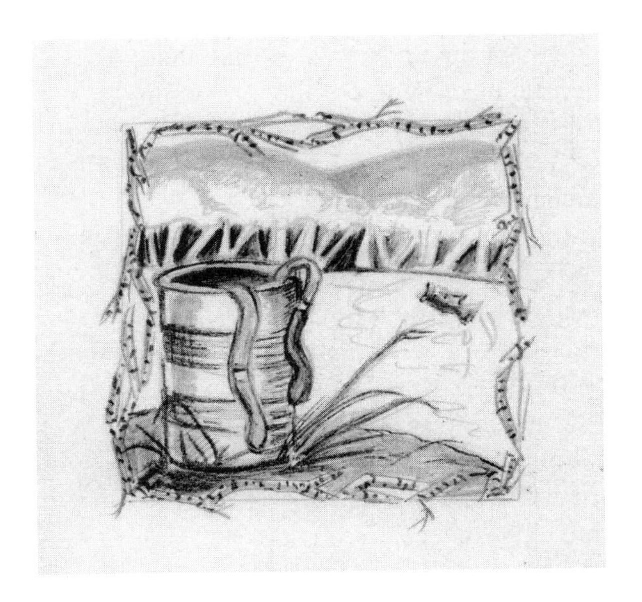

THE LARGE MOUTH

Della had spread clothes from the Shearcott's basket onto the table and draped them over the backs of chairs. When WC came in from chores she was holding a velvety jacket against her cheek.

"These are some kind of clothes. This here feels as soft as hair on a new calf."

"Can you imagine what thirty minutes in the barn would do to it?"

"It's not meant for working in. Wear it to church tomorrow."

"I'll wear what I always wear."

"Why do you have to be so contrary?"

"I didn't ask for them and I don't have any use for them—except the underwear. I like them; they fit, but I feel a little naked without the long johns."

"I'm saving everything for special times. Who knows?" She began folding and laying the clothes back into the basket.

"I might wear some of those things to a funeral, but that would be the only place."

"Well, I want you to hurry and eat breakfast." His place was cleared of the clothes and she pulled the chair out for him.

"I want you to ride over to Clair's—"

"Ma, I planned to cut firewood, clean the stalls and manure the melon field, before I leave. Why do you want me to go there?"

"I want you to invite them for Sunday dinner with us."

"What for?"

"If you're leaving, you need some family to send you off."

* * * * *

WC rode Kate bareback to the bottom land where he found his Aunt Clair sitting on the edge of the porch rocking her squalling baby. Tommy Irene was inside washing a mountain of dishes and did not answer his greeting. He sat beside Clair and tickled his finger in the neck of the infant.

"Hey, looky here." The baby stopped crying, gazed wide-eyed at the new voice, grimaced, and cried again.

"He's still colicky." Clair rubbed his stomach. "Nothing will ease his poor little tummy, and he's driving me crazy—crying all the time. Carol Beth, hold Emmett for me, while I rest." She held him out to her youngest daughter.

"I don't want to hold him," the little girl whined.

Clair snapped at her. "Take him so I can talk with WC and get the crick out of my arms. And if you say one word more, I'll slap your jaws."

She stood, raised her arms and stretched. It was the same tired movement his mother made when she needed to recover from a wearying activity. It must be the sister in them, he thought.

"Tommy Irene, c'mon out and say hello."

Tommy wore her mother's apron slouching to her toes. She dried her hands on a dishtowel and pretended WC was not there.

"Make Carol Beth help me with dishes. She never lifts a hand to anything."

"She's holding the baby."

"I don't want to hold the baby."

"I'll hold the baby. Let her wet her hands for a change."

"No!" Carol hugged the child tightly to her body. "Dishes is your job."

"According to you, all the jobs are mine." She dug at Carol's arms and the baby howled.

Clair slapped both girls.

"Quit wrestling with that child. Can't either of you give me a moment's rest?" She laid Emmett over her shoulder, patting his back. The tiny body stiffened with another cramp and he screamed into her ear. It must make her deaf, WC thought.

"Where are Uncle Block and the boys?" WC had to almost shout.

Tommy laughed. "Bill Philip and James would beat your butt if they heard you call them 'boys.' "

"They're down in the woods." Clair jostled the baby. "They won't be back for a while."

"They're making a delivery in Des Arc tonight," Carol nodded conspiratorially.

Both Clair and Tommy turned on her, told her to shut her mouth and shoved her inside. WC had overheard conversations that rumored Uncle Block was mixed up in the whiskey trade.

Tommy pulled the apron off over her head.

"What you doing here, anyways?"

"Ma sent me to invite you all for dinner tomorrow."

Clair switched the baby to her other ear.

"She did? What for?"

WC held his hands out for the child.

"Let me spell you, Aunt Clair."

"You want to go with Cousin Warren?" She laid the yowling infant in WC's arms.

"Hush, little peanut. You're all right." He began shushing and swaying Emmett gently.

"I got me a job at a logging camp. I start out Monday and Ma wanted the family for a good-bye supper."

"You got a job, sure enough?" Clair tried to keep the note of envy out of her voice, but it was unmistakable and she was sure he could hear it.

"Good for you, WC, I'm happy for you."

"I'll have to put up in the bunkhouse with the other men, and the boss says we work dawn to dark." The baby was quieting and squeezed WC's offered little finger.

"Huh," Tommy huffed. " 'With the other men?' Including yourself, aren't you?"

She looked past WC, out into the scrubby land.

"Here comes Jimmy. And he's mad about something."

Clair shaded her eyes.

"I wonder what he's up to?"

Tommy drew her mother aside, stood on tip toe and whispered in her ear. Clair turned to look back at WC as he hummed to the now silent baby. She bent down to her daughter's ear. The girl whooped, threw the apron in the air, caught it and ran into the house.

Clair shook her head at WC.

"Looks like you're magic with babies." She kissed his cheek. "I'm proud of you."

"I've got work at home. I just came to ask you to supper." He laid the exhausted baby in her arms.

"All right. I don't want to hold you up, but could you wait for Tommy Irene to clear off the dishes? She sure would like to go back home with you and spend the night. She loves her Aunt Della, and Della loves spoiling a girl. Unless you think she would be in the way."

WC glanced at the door and saw a patch of red hair pull back into the shadows. He cringed at the thought of having her around for the whole day. Suddenly, though, she was singing. He heard her over the dishes clattering and water sloshing.

"You know Ma always has a welcome for her. I believe she had something like that in her mind when she sent me over."

"Look at him stomp, will you? I wonder what that's all about." WC turned to watch Jimmy approach, but when he waved and Jimmy recognized WC, he veered off and ran for the woods.

* * * * *

Della was delighted to have Tommy, and as soon as she arrived they went arm in arm inside the house to have coffee together. WC went to the barn to clean the stalls. Just as he was ready to pitch manure onto the wagon, Della and Tommy walked out to announce dinner.

"What did you do to your hair?"

"Aunt Della brushed and brushed it, stupid. And then she tied it up in ribbon. So there."

He wanted to put the pitchfork in her tongue, but stabbed it instead into the reeking pile.

"Looks nice. Grown up."

"What would you know about it?"

"Sweetie, take it for a compliment. They come precious few in our lives. WC, wash up and let's eat."

After dinner, WC took the fishing poles from the barn and dug worms to fill a can—Della wanted fish for supper. WC protested he did not have time, but he loved fishing as much as hunting and was easily persuaded to postpone what work he thought he needed to do until later.

"It won't take you long to string our supper, and my mouth is set for fish. How about you, pretty little girl, you ready for fish?"

"It would take half the time if I went along to help."

WC groaned inwardly.

* * * * *

They fished in quiet concentration. It was unusual for her to be so focused and determined. She had made it clear she was not interested in catching 'measly ole pan fish,' she was after something bigger—large-mouth bass, maybe. From a fallen log half submerged up the river, WC watched her lift and swing her bait from spot to spot, hardly giving the fish a chance to catch a smell. She hummed and sang to herself. WC thought about Emmett's everlasting crying and all the dishes she had done. He was glad she had come.

"Got any bites?" He called to her.

"I thought you said there were fish here?" She was tired of unmet expectation and jabbed the end of her pole into the mud. She sat behind it and drew her knees up to her chest.

"I've caught six." He lifted a rope from the stream. Water spilled off the fish crammed on one end of it.

"You're such a show off."

"I told you that spot would not be good for action, but it is the best place for catching something big. You're doing the right thing now, by leaving your bait still."

"I know what I'm doing. Don't think I ain't ever wet a line before."

"Whoa, got me another." WC set the hook and began bringing a fish to his outstretched hand. Tommy Irene stood to watch.

"That's another nice one."

"Well, if you want to come up here, I'll give you my spot."

"No, I'll rest my hope in catching a big bass, and let you pick up all the itty-bitty ones." The woods grew quiet as she let the water pass through her fingers and watched WC catch three more fish.

Though he enjoyed the peace, WC wondered about Tommy Irene's unexpected behavior: why she became so involved in shredding a leaf or peeling the bark off a twig, and what seemed to absorb her as she held her pant legs up and watched the river run over her feet. It simply was not the usual Tommy Irene he knew. Finally she spoke, but even then she seemed out of character—open, receptive.

"How come you to take baby Emmett in your arms this morning? All he does is bawl all the time."

"I don't know. Seemed a help to Aunt Clair, I guess. Why?"

"It was nice." She stooped and swished her hand in the water.

"Things get plumb crazy around the house. Sometimes, I can hardly stand to—Lord, almighty!" She sprang away from the water and stood.

The end of Tommy Irene's pole had twitched, then throbbed, bent, and was now being dragged into the river. She grabbed the handle just before it slid under water.

"WC! Quick!" The pole arched and bobbed and the line zinged a speeding track of spray. Tommy pulled and grunted against a great fish.

"Not so hard, Irene. Don't horse it. You'll break it off." He stood beside her, patting her shoulder.

"You're doing good. You got yourself a big one."

She giggled and her tongue was half way out of her mouth.

"Keep the pole high—let him tire out."

The fish swirled to the surface and broke the water, shaking its head.

"Oh, my God! Oh, my God!"

"It's huge, Irene. Did you see it? It's a hog."

"I don't want to lose it. I don't want to lose it."

"Back up, slow—bring it to the bank. Slowly and I'll get it."

She strained at the live tugging weight roiling against her.

"Do you see it?"

"Nice and slow. There it comes."

"Don't let it get away!"

"He's tiring."

"Get it! Please, oh please."

The fish grounded to the shallows and WC ran his finger under its gill plate and lifted it. Tommy dropped the pole and ran to the river's edge. WC threw the hook and line back into the water and handed Tommy the fish.

"I caught the biggest bass in all of Arkansas. That mouth is big enough to put your head into. I love you. I love you. I love you." She kissed it between the eyes and laid her cheek against its slimy scales.

WC hugged her with one arm.

"I love it!" She shouted and held it to the heavens.

"What a monster, Irene. You want me to string it for you?"

She frowned and pulled it away from his hands. She cradled the fish to her chest and sat down crying.

"What's wrong? Did the dang thing, fin you?"

"No-ooo. It's not hurt me-eee." She sobbed and shook.

She was the most pathetic and anguished sight he had ever seen. He thought about rubbing her back, but instead told her she would be all right.

"That's the happiest thing ever happen to me."

"And it made you cry?"

"I don't know. It's just stupid. Dumb, dumb, dumb."

"What's dumb?"

"Well, for one thing, you calling me 'Irene.' You ain't ever done that before. For another, why should I be so happy over this ol' fish?"

She held it away from her, so they were eye to eye.

"I won't let no one hurt you. I ain't killing you. I'm going to put you back."

"Put it back? You crazy? A fish that big?"

She squeezed it to her chest; its eyes bugged and jaws gasped, and a string of slime connected her chin with the fish.

"I'm not going to reward him my happiness with a frying pan."

"Well, you better hurry then, before he smothers."

She squatted and petted the slab-sided fish to the water. She held it there until its tail swung back and forth.

"Go on and hide. Don't let no one else catch you but me." The fish burst away, its thrust stirring the shallows into a cloud.

It must have carried something of Tommy Irene off with it, for as the aroused mud settled, she was free herself. Given the gift of such a fish, so unexpectedly, relieved all her fears and defenses—made them worthless and defeating. And there was the surprise that WC had used her middle name, her feminine name, during the excitement of landing the fish. How would he know that was important to her? Only Aunt Della and the teacher used that form. When that fish swam away, when she gave it life, there was an opening for her to trust, and she was bursting to unburden herself.

Tommy Irene rinsed her slippery hands in the water and looked back at WC.

"I don't want to fish anymore."

"All right, we can go back. I have enough for supper."

"No, I want to sit a while." She stood and pointed back at a grassy spot where the bank began to rise.

"You can stay, but I have to get back and finish my work."

"Go on and do your ol' work then."

He could tell she was disappointed.

"You caught a great fish."

"You going to leave me alone with snakes and spiders? Aunt Della won't like you doing that." She sat on the grass.

He really did not want to be bothered, but he hesitated—she looked hopelessly resigned, slumped over her pole, winding the fishing line around its tip.

"I guess it won't hurt to stay a little longer." He went back up river to where he had dropped his pole.

"Could you sit down here, so I don't have to talk so far?"

He sat beside her and together they finished wrapping their lines. She dug in the worm can sitting between them, taking one out and laying it in the palm of her hand. It stretched full length and wriggled until it fell off to the ground.

"I got a boy friend."

"All you girls at school got boy friends. But none care about you, except to pull your hair."

"This is a real boy friend. He ain't from school." She looked at WC and smiled, but had to wipe a fast flowing tear off her cheek.

"What's the matter? What are you crying about now?"

"I want to tell you something, but you first have to promise not to tell any body. Promise?"

"Why would I tell?"

She grabbed his arm with both hands.

"Ow. Not so hard."

"You got to promise, first."

"That hurts! All right, let go, I promise."

"Is that the truth?"

"I promised didn't I?"

She searched his eyes before she put her hands into her lap and stared at them. He rubbed the red mark she had made on his arm.

"It's Dar Davis."

"What about him?"

"He's my boy friend."

"No he's not. He's too old—Bill Philip's age."

"Older. He's twenty-one. Asked me if I wanted to be his secret sweetheart. I said I thought it was a good idea."

" 'A good idea!' " WC could not sit still with the thought. He walked away and drove a stone into the water before he turned back to look at her. She made him think of something broken—a little stump with twigs struggling to grow from its roots. He gathered a handful of stones and brought them back to her.

'What's wrong? Has he hurt you?"

She listlessly tossed a stone, "kerplunk," into the river.

"No, he scares me though. He used to hold my hand, and I liked that. But then he wanted to kiss."

WC slung a stone rattling in the trees arching over the river.

"On the cheek was ok, but, you know, the lips–"

"You didn't let him, did you?"

"... Just once was all."

"You've got to tell him to leave you alone, or he won't quit with just kissing."

"I know. He says he thinks I would look real good without my clothes on."

"Dang it!" WC heaved the can of worms at the river. The worms and dirt spilled out, separated, and sizzled into the water.

"I keep them on. I ain't stupid, you know."

"You've got to tell Aunt Clair."

"I can't do that. She'll whip me."

" 'Whip you?' What for?"

"For being dirty."

"You're not the one 'being dirty.' It's him. She'll most likely kill him."

"I don't want to make trouble. We have enough of that already."

"My Lord, he's the one who's made the trouble—not you. Do you want that son-of-a-gun to keep doing what he's doing?"

"No." She rolled to her stomach and hid her face in her hands.

"Well, then tell your ma."

"Bill Philip and Jimmy know. They caught him once holding my hand and sweet-talking me behind the house."

"Did they tell?"

"No. They didn't do nothing but laugh."

"They're your brothers—they should be helping you."

Tommy Irene shook her head.

"Well, dang it, Aunt Clair should know something's not right, if he's coming around dogging you all the time. And if she doesn't know, you have to tell her."

"No, and you don't either. You promised." She scrambled up and stood in front of him.

"Then why did you tell me?"

"I've been holding back until I was almost busted wide open. I had to tell someone, and who would that be?"

"Tell my ma—I'll tell her for you."

"If Aunt Della thinks I'm like that, I'll die."

"You're not 'like that.' No one thinks you are."

"Everyone would be ashamed of me, and I already feel bad enough."

"You haven't done anything to be ashamed of."

"Yes, I did. I said I'd be his 'secret sweetheart.' "

"He shouldn't have asked."

She shook a finger at him.

"I told you, Warren Carl Thomas, because I knew you wouldn't break a promise."

"But it's not your fault. He's the one who knows better and is using you like a fool."

She grabbed the straps of his overalls and shook him.

"Don't you dare tell! Don't you ever tell anyone."

He grabbed her and shook right back.

"Dang that Dar Davis! Dang those worthless brothers and your mother for not seeing what's right in front of her eyes! And dang you for feeling guilty and keeping quiet."

She released him and he released her.

"Thanks, WC."

"Tell him you don't want to be his girl friend anymore."

"I did. It didn't help."

CHAPTER TWELVE

THE WAGER

It was all WC could do to eat at the same table with Aunt Clair and Jimmy. They had come with Carol Elizabeth and baby Emmett right after church. Jimmy was still acting angry from yesterday; Uncle Block and Bill Philip had left him behind while they went to Des Arc. WC did not miss his uncle and he cared less if he ever saw Bill Philip again. He resented the entire family for not protecting Tommy Irene. Clair tried several times to get WC to warm up to her, but he remained cool and unanswering the entire time she was there. It was her job to know Dar Davis had his eye on her daughter.

Della was disappointed with his behavior and spoke to him about rudeness. He did not care and shrugged her off as well.

Tommy Irene was not herself either. She avoided WC, stayed close to the women and, for once, had little to say.

Jimmy followed WC everywhere, badgering, trying to pick a fight. He bragged about making whiskey, how much of it he drank, and how much he smoked. WC wanted to oblige him the fight, but he was company and more provocation was needed than his stupid needling. When Jimmy wanted to go fishing and "catch one bigger than Tommy Irene's lie," WC was more than happy to give him a pole and be free of him. He was able to sit in the barn to shave and smooth a piece of hickory he had cut for his ax handle.

When it was time for Clair and the kids to leave, Della sent WC to find Jimmy. He walked to the river hating every step he took out of his way for that boy who did not know to protect his own sister. At the edge of the woods, he began calling for him.

"Jim-meeee. C'mon, your ma's ready to leave."

He thought, "He'll make me traipse all over these woods, hollering myself hoarse, and there he'll be, back at the house, laughing at me.

Down the river he heard a voice calling.

"Help! Someone, quick!"

It was Jimmy.

"It's biting me! Come and help me."

WC ran toward the panicked shouting. He jumped logs and whipped through branches in the way.

"Hurry, hurry. Do something—get it off."

WC fell, smashing his knee onto the hard clay, but he limped on to where he saw Jimmy standing knee deep in water, holding one of his legs. WC splashed to where Jimmy thrashed wildly.

"It swam up my pant leg! I can't get it out. I can't get it to turn loose."

Something long and round bulged under his pant leg. Jimmy frantically pulled at it through his trousers.

"It's a cotton mouth!"

WC dragged him to the bank. Jimmy fell back screaming. The bulge fell to the inside of Jimmy's leg.

"I'll get it—hold still."

He reached up the pant leg and felt something wet and slick. He did not know which end he had, but he grabbed and pulled it out.

Jimmy began laughing. He rolled on the bank pointing at the waterlogged stick WC held in his hand.

"Made you come galloping, didn't I? Splashed in the water for a sorry ol' stick."

He mocked WC.

"Oh, you should have seen yourself. 'I'll get it—hold still.' " He kicked his legs into the air and pounded the ground with uncontained laughter.

It took WC a moment to realize it had been a prank and he had been cruelly tricked. What he had feared might kill him, the thing he had risked his life to remove, was nothing but a sopped dead weight. It did not loop back and bite him, but was inert, logged with water and tough. It was then he felt his pounding heart and throbbing knee.

Jimmy turned over and rose to his hands and knees, but another thought and fit of laughter caused the upper part of his body to bow to the ground.

"Wait till I tell Bill Philip about this."

His backside was presented high into the air, exposed, an irresistible temptation. WC was well aware that beneath the rounding denim of Jimmy's trousers there was a soft cleft target begging for retribution. WC raised the serpent-stick and whacked it across the blue-mooning butt before him. It made a lovely crack.

" 'It's a cotton mouth,' Jimmy!"

Jimmy straightened up, his mouth and eyes wide in shock and disbelief. Another good stroke and he grabbed his smarting cheeks, yowling. The snake bit him across the hands. Jimmy pushed up to stand and the snake stuck its fangs into his butt again. He wailed and ran for the house.

* * * * *

WC struggled with his promise to Tommy Irene. He wanted to do the right thing—keep his promise. But to do that, the wrong thing might happen—she might be hurt. So doing the right thing might be wrong. The right thing, then, would be to tell someone so she would get some help. It would be wrong, though, to break the trust. He figured he could do most anything a man could do, but carrying another's misery, without any power over it, made him feel more like a little boy than facing forty acres of unplowed ground. Worrying what he should do, and fuming at the family's blind eye toward Tommy Irene, kept him awake most of the night. He could not tell anyone—he could not not tell anyone.

Della had to wake him. She fried slices of ham, eggs, and made sandwiches of them. He was not hungry, "too excited" Della had suspected, but he ate one sandwich and saved the other for his walk to the camp. Della relieved her misgivings by chattering away with gossip about Brother Ramsey's preaching, the "disgraceful singing of some people—who shall remain nameless," and how much Michael, the new rooster, was "next to Gabriel when it came to pure ornery."

"And Custer will likely come dragging back in today—all sick and useless. With you gone as his slave, he'll never do the chores or the farm work himself. I can see it all, right now. He'll sit at this table, rehearsing everything, getting up his courage, and then go whining to his brother that 'the boy run off, left his responsibilities, and the farm's going to fail if we don't hire a hand.' "

WC had little response to her ramblings, especially those referring to old Dedge. He swallowed the last of his coffee and pushed himself away from the table. He looked at his place, patted his chair and internally gave it "good-bye." Everything was ready, lined up at the door: his bundle of clothes, the 22 rifle fitted with a leather sling he had made for it, and the ax.

Della walked with him to the bottom of the drive.

"It won't be light for three hours or so. You be careful."

"I will."

"If you come back like them men you're working with, you'll get the worst whipping you ever had."

"Don't worry, that strap will be safe with me." He stopped, set the clothes down and shifted the rifle.

"What is it? Are you having second thoughts?"

"No. I've been thinking about you and Tommy Irene. You get along together."

"I do enjoy the life in that girl, and giving her what she does not get at home."

"Aunt Clair uses her pretty hard. Those boys count for nothing and Carol Beth isn't much help either. There's all those strange men showing up there all the time. Who knows what all. Everything lands on Tommy Irene. It doesn't seem fair."

"You're right; she's a lot on her shoulders."

"I was thinking you should spend more time together. She could stay a night or two, keep company and you'd be able to doll her up all you wanted. Just think about all the things you could talk about: church, clothes, boy friends. It would be a good thing for both of you; I'd sure feel better. She could go to school from here. Why don't you ride over one morning, visit Aunt Clair, and bring Tommy Irene back with you—keep her a while."

"That's a good idea. I'll see about doing it."

"Don't wait. Do it real soon."

He reached down for the bundle of clothes and began backing away.

"I'll be home after dark on Saturday to check on you. I'll sleep in the barn, unless we're lucky and old Dedge is gone for good."

"Don't forget to tell your bosses about the family gathering at your Uncle Otis'. They may let you off early, if you ask. It's in two weeks, remember." She waved as he began fading into the dark.

"If you want to know where that dandelion seed is, it's right here." He put the head of the ax against the breast pocket of his overalls. He turned and marched into the morning dark.

* * * * *

Roy took little notice of him when he came into camp. He turned him over to Frank, the woods foreman, and went back to writing on his pad. The rifle was locked in the shed and WC was led to the bunkhouse. It reeked of tobacco and the odor of hard-working men living close together with no energy or enthusiasm left over for bathing or laundering. A kerosene lantern flickered shadows of barrenness. No tables, no chairs, just fourteen beds—four bunks head to toe against one wall, three against another and an aisle in between. The only life in this building was spent in sleep. WC had the feeling of an overworked field; everything leached from it, forsaken.

Frank assigned him a bed, told him to "shake a leg, the woods are waiting," and left. WC threw the bundle of clothes on the foot of the top bunk and sat on the bed below to put on his shoes and socks. A hacking cough rasped from the rear corner. An arm and leg flopped over the edge of the upper mattress and shook with another racking spell of coughing. The man stopped long enough to gather thick phlegm and spit somewhere. He cursed the day, swung himself to the edge of the bed and looked down at the skinny kid below. WC pulled hurriedly at his laces.

Heavy boots—brogans most likely—thudded against the raw timbered floor. A sneering voice boomed.

"Boy, git yer unwiped behind off my bunk."

"I was just tying my shoes." He glanced to see a stout, powerfully built man with a dark beard and moustache.

"GIT OFF MY BUNK!"

WC dropped to the floor, as fast as he could get there. He ducked and the shoes clomped over him. They were brogans all right.

The man leaned against the back bunk.

"Albert, ya'll be sorry ya didn't eat some breakfast."

"I ain't up to eating, Hurley. I'm sick." He let his shoulders slump even lower onto his scrawny body.

"Yer always sick. Let me tell ya, if ya miss another day of work, they'll fill yer bunk with someone else." He looked at WC.

"Most likely another droopy-drawers like that one." He cursed. Not just once or twice, either. He hung his swearing into a flapping clothesline.

"Ya coming, or ain't ya? The tool wagon's leaving."

Albert hung his balding head, wagged it, whining.

"I don't believe I can make it. Be all right by tomorrow."

Hurley pulled him off the bunk.

"If ya don't work, they'll probably partner me with that scrawny brat. If ya weren't my sister's husband, I'd leave ya here to get fired."

WC grabbed his ax, hurried from the building to follow a group of men moving silently into the woods. Looking back, he saw Hurley and Albert straggling behind.

* * * * *

The foreman set WC to touching up saw blades and axes: a job that kept him out of the way, both of the men and of the real work of logging. It was unsatisfying and almost intolerable when he watched the men notch a tree. He aspired to that ax work as they chopped a deep gash into one side of the tree, determining the direction in which it would fall. They would break through the bark with upward swings across one side of a tree. Then they would chop downward strokes to meet against the row below, opening a gap. WC offered to start trees, but the men brushed him aside. No one would let him touch his ax to a tree.

He did, however, use his ax when he was made to drive the steel wedge while two men were sawing. It was driven into their cut and levered the tree off the saw, keeping it free to be pulled back and forth. Once its blade had sliced far enough toward the notch on the opposite side, the tree would topple. He hated doing it because the ax head took such punishment beating against the hunk of steel. He was afraid it would eventually mutilate the tool he had put such effort into for cutting, not for sledging.

Roy had predicted the men would not treat WC any differently than they treated each other, but he had not said they were going to treat him worse. Amongst themselves they played coarse jokes or worked in silence. But for him, there were only bitter words or abuse.

He tried to anticipate their needs and moves, but everyone was different. Their reactions, however, were the same—they complained and cussed him out. He did it too soon, too late, too slow, or too fast. Nothing was to their liking.

"You call this sharp? Couldn't cut Cookie's corn bread."

Another man answered. "Nothing's sharp enough to cut Cookie's corn bread."

Halfway through the day, WC felt he had a dozen old Dedges snapping at his heels. He did not understand their resentment or feel it deserved; he kept his mouth shut, though. He had a job and he would be paid for it. Someday, if they gave him a chance to work with his ax, he would show he belonged.

Already he had noticed a certain admiration they had for his ax. He caught one man thumbing its edge and testing its weight by swinging it like a hatchet.

"Where did you get this here ax?"

"Found it."

"Found it like this?"

"No, sir. I put the edge on it and cut me the handle."

"Won't hold up to any real work."

"I believe it will. It's made for my weight and reach. You want to put it down, please."

“Yeah, sure enough.” He chopped it into the dirt—a sure way to dull it.

* * * * *

He thought he knew what work was and what it felt like to be tired. But the way everyone had dogged and ground at him, he was ready to sleep right after supper. Most of the men stayed at the table smoking. They did nothing but argue and complain. WC left his place at the end of the table and went outside.

“One day. I’ve done one day.”

He saw the moon overhead, so he sat against the cook house wall to watch it and try to work the cramps out of his hands and neck. He laid the ax across his lap, the fresh, new handle darkened from his sweat and oils. He could still feel the pinch in his neck, and the shock to his shoulders and hands, as the back of the head drove the heavy chunk of wedge-shaped metal into the slice the men were sawing into the tree. He had given no consideration to his ax doing that kind of work. It was not made for slamming against steel, and its striking tinking sound was almost comical to the enormity of the task of lifting that tree away from the cutter’s saw blade. He remembered Albert, the coughing man, being the worse all day for finding fault with him.

“Swing, dang you, boy! Git that wedge in deeper. Why don’t you use a real tool—not some toy? If this tree pinches our saw, I’ll kick those ears off your head.”

Cookie cussed the stragglers out the dining house door and most of them spit and flicked cigarettes into the air on their way to the bunkhouse. WC continued to sit, wait for the other men to settle. He passed the file over the ax's edge so he could "get something for his weariness."

Not once all day had he used its edge, and he yearned to test his resurrected tool—swing it against something living, something giving, that would spray and pile at his feet and prove his worthiness. The wretched blunt hammering humiliated his best efforts in the filing he had done.

He needed a sledge but that was hopeless, for they were nearly as big as he was and too heavy. He would have to make one or end up ruining his ax. There was a busted maul in the tool wagon. Its head was lighter than the sledge but made for heavier work than an ax. He could use the head from it.

Frank, the foreman, saw him and stopped.

"Why you carrying that ax everywhere? I worried at supper you were planning on chopping the legs off the table."

"No, sir. I just don't want to lose track of it."

"Let me have a look. The men have been talking about it." WC watched as he rubbed his hand over the tapered head, sighted down the handle's length, and then cut the edge against his thumbnail.

"That's smart work, you done." Frank returned the ax.

"Don't worry about the other men. You did well today. Better than I thought. Go on to bed, now. Get some rest."

* * * * *

He was awake and up before everyone else that first morning. He had found a suitable oak limb in one of the brush piles and was cutting, shaving and shaping it into a handle. When Frank found out it was for the broken maul he told him to finish it and then follow them to the woods.

The rehandled maul made driving the wedge something he was much more adequate for, even though some of the workmen ridiculed his grunts and gasps at his final strokes. But he was catching on quickly, learning the work and habits of the different men. But after three days, still no one had let him work with his ax, and he was aching to prove himself with it. He took a chance while working with Albert and Hurley.

"Mr. Hurley, might I have a try at notching this tree?" He stood facing the tree, legs spread, ax held ready.

"Droopy Drawers, we have so many trees to cut a day; we git in trouble if we don't. So we ain't got time for ya to hack with that hatchet. Tell you what ya can do, though. Go cut the weeds around the cook house. Now step back out of the way; let a man do his work."

Albert shoved WC aside.

"Yeah, ya heard him. Git out of the way." He struck a line into the tree and another about twelve inches below it.

"Them's the notch marks, Little Blue Britches. Think that little hatchet's gonna do more than wound this poor ol' tree? I don't even know what they got ya here for. Best ya find yer mommy's titty and stay out from under men's feet."

"I'll wager I can notch this one by myself, before the two of you can finish that one over there."

Albert cackled and wiped the sweat from his balding head.

"He'll wet his shoes, won't he, Brother, peeing in the wind that way."

"I'll bet my day's wage I can do it." He wiped his nose on the sleeve of his long johns.

"Whichever way it turns out, you have two trees notched for the price of one. You going to laugh yourselves silly or take my money?"

Albert put his hand on Hurley's broad shoulder.

"Come on, let's go knock this tree down on top of Little Blue Britches." They tramped to the tree.

Hurley, the stronger and better woodsmen of the two, set his feet in front of the tree, rubbed his hands together, and blustered to WC.

"Hey, hound's breath. We might just drop this tree right on yer head. Yeah, we'll peg ya into the ground."

Albert jeered. "Won't no one find anything of ya, but a knot of black hair. We'll even give ya the first swing. Go on ahead."

WC blew on his hands, took aim at the low mark and swung. The blade spit bark and sank deeply, to where the steel widened out, curling a thick plug of wood away. It levered out easily and he was right back into a swing. And then another. A white smile leered along the lower mark. The ax swung and returned as if it bounced off the tree, each bite burying itself the full depth of the filed, tapered head. A chunk of wood popped off and flew over his head.

The top mark was too high for him to have any leverage. He ran to a tool crate, dumped it out and carried it back to the tree. It was unstable and wobbled, his strokes into the tree were loaded with little more than arm and shoulder muscles. But the upper mark was ruptured and a white eyebrow became obvious. He kicked the crate aside with his leg and exploded into the lower gash. The ax made a cracking sound, bursting chips and hunks into the air. He worked to the end of the mark, cleaning away the loosened chunks and then worked back to cleave a new cut. He replaced the crate and heard Hurley and Albert laughing and joking. His confidence grew. They rarely had their tools sharpened and Albert was, by far, the worst ax man on the whole crew. What made him so bad with the ax was that he thought he was so good with it. WC counted on his delusion.

WC worked across the lower line again and the smile and eyebrow were joined into a single white socket. The upper and lower lines were clean and deeply angled to meet at the core of the tree. Debris cluttered at the base and WC had to keep clearing space to set his feet.

Other men of the crew began gathering as they heard Albert's yelping boasts and realized a contest was underway. They warned Hurley and Albert they had better speed up. Then the betting began.

Every time anyone put money on WC, Albert chopped a curse into the tree. The foreman, Frank, did not make a bet, but he allowed the race to continue. The few men who took WC shouted encouragement. The others worried in silence, growing less certain about their wager against the boy.

Hurley brushed imbedded wood chips from his beard and moustache, as he strode over to check on the little runt's progress. He took one look at WC's work and ran back hollering at Albert.

"Lay on that ax. Quit pitty-patting, and bite into that tree." They began arguing.

"Out of my way. You're hopeless. Couldn't chop a clean line if yer life depended on it."

"My line's straight as yer's."

"Ya call that straight? I said git back. Anyone who whacks an ax as deep as ya do might just as well use a jackknife."

Frank elbowed the man next to him.

"Have you seen that boy's ax, Pokey? He's got that head shaved so far back it don't take much more than a boy to put a man's bite into a tree."

"Yep, I know. Saw that danged tool yesterday. I figured it could cut. But look at the skill. He hits where he aims and he knows just where to send the next stroke." Pokey hollered at the boy.

"Lay into it! Give it some hip!" He nudged his boss.

"I put twenty-five cents on him. Well, really, I put twenty-five cents against Albert."

Men who bet against WC were converted by his desire. They shouted cheers, suggestions, and cussed Albert and Hurley, who worked in a panic and were heart-rending.

WC was up and down, across and back like a mechanical woodpecker. But he was obviously winded and had to stop. He dropped the ax, bent over and held his knees. The men all groaned in disappointment.

WC heard them for the first time and looked up. He was surprised to see them all gathered, away from their work.

They told him not to quit—that he had a chance. He flexed his arms, shook out his hands, pulled one leg to his chest and then the other. Everyone laughed and cheered when he dropped his overalls and kicked them out of the way.

He looked at Frank and explained.

"This pair is too small. They're binding my swing."

Pokey shouted, "Take off them long johns, if you have to."

When he spit on his hands and grabbed the ax, the men all cheered. He deepened the lower cut: a toothy white grin smiling off a wood spirit. Standing on the crate, he knocked the teeth out of the top mark. Gnarled molars sprayed to the ground. He had become a flailing devil, in faded long underwear, pursuing the soul of the tree. He ignored the chips which stuck like ticks in his hair, while the notch angled deeper into the life-circles.

Someone shouted, "He's hit heartwood. C'mon, boy, you're almost there."

Albert ran over to see.

"He's gotta be a third of the way through. A third through, I tell ya. We're into heartwood, and he took a head start on us."

The men all laughed and mocked as Albert ran back, cussing Hurley to hurry.

The race looked dead even and generated more excitement from the men than Frank had ever seen.

There was a problem though. What if WC won? What would he gain? Would it really be in his best interest? It seemed to the foreman the boy had already made enough of a statement and anything more might do more damage than good.

Hurley stopped to compare their notch to the rest of the tree.

"We've done it! We're notched!"

A few men, the heaviest bettors, agreed with him. But most said they had a way to go yet. Frank stepped in.

"Hurley, you and Albert can call it quits. You won."

The two men whooped and danced and Albert raised Hurley's arm. The other men discussed their debts and nudged each other shoulders about the disputed victory. But everyone slowly grew quiet as the woods continued to crack with the sound of a chopping ax.

Chunks of wood flew from WC's tree. A frenzied demon snarled and growled at the end of the ax. Its wild black hair whipped and flung sweat. A beast sent straight up from burning Hell had ravaged the boy.

The men gathered behind their foreman. Preachers had warned them of devil possession. Someone had to do something. Someone had to save the boy. Frank shouted at him.

"Warren! That's enough."

The slashing and snarling continued.

"I said you're done. The tree's notched."

Frank stepped closer.

"Stand back from the tree. You've notched it—leave the rest for the saw."

He answered with wildness—such blinding wildness he missed his aim and broke the handle at the neck, sending the head flying free. He held the decapitated tool before him, bewildered, and then slung it away. He dropped to his knees panting for breath.

As the air slowly cleared of fire and brimstone, the men began to silently, reluctantly make their way back to work. One man picked up the dismembered ax head and handed it off to Frank. Frank carried it to WC and stooped beside him.

"Here's your ax. Sorry it busted."

WC slowly looked up and took it from him.

"There's plenty more hickory handles around." He examined the ax, turning it over and over.

"I lost. Didn't ever expect I would."

"Who's to say what losing is? You lost the race, but I think you may have won a lot more than that today." The woods boss nudged his shoulder, stood up and hollered for everyone to get back to work.

"Catch your breath a while, then join us." He walked away telling Hurley and Albert to have WC sharpen their axes.

Pokey ambled up and dropped WC's overalls beside him.

"You cost me twenty-five cents today, kid." He shook a finger at WC. "And you were worth every penny of it. Welcome to camp."

CHAPTER THIRTEEN

THE HUNT

The first weekend WC spent back home with Della, she had said Tommy Irene had not been able to stay over with her, as Clair could not spare the girl from the many chores. He almost broke his promise right then and told about Dar Davis' improper attention toward the younger girl. But, instead, he again pressed the need for his mother to have the two of them get together, even for a matter of a few hours if that was all that could be managed. He emphasized the need for girls to talk to each other, and told her to be sure to try again—soon. The dilemma and guilt of his promise to Tommy Irene tormented him. His mother had to uncover her niece's danger; every day was a threat. As he saw it, Della was God's best hope for the girl's safety. He was a miserable failure and could not save anyone.

It was Friday, the end of WC's second week of work, and everyone except Albert and Hurley had eased up on him. The men trusted their tools to him more, and often times he was called on to help notch or limb a fallen tree. He had nothing to complain about or wish for—"Everything was humming along," as he had overheard Frank tell Roy.

WC sat at breakfast doing his fair share of eating, reaching for another biscuit every time the platter came near. He felt hungry nearly all the time. Cookie burst out of his kitchen, roared up to Roy and began berating him with a long handled spatula.

"I'm tired of the complaints and tired of insults. I'm sick of cooking the same ol' thing everyday. What's the challenge to beans and pork?"

The men at the table cheered.

"Good heavenly days, these men will fart themselves to death. I don't suppose you hired me because I'm so good at identifying poison ivy and warning your men away from it. No! You hired me because I was good at cooking. You need to give me something to work with or find someone else to do it. I'm bored to death—even the pots and pans are rebelling."

Roy motioned Cookie to calm down.

"I haven't been able to spare a man for hunting."

Cookie untied the strings to his apron.

"That's it then! Maybe you can spare one of them for cooking. We'll see how you like that." He balled the apron up and threw it on the floor.

"Put your apron back on, Cookie. I'll get someone out hunting this morning."

Roy stood and looked down both sides of the table. He stopped when he came to Hurley.

"Where's Albert?"

"In his bunk."

"Is he going to work today?"

"Says he's too sick."

"Frank." The camp boss interrupted the foreman's sip of coffee.

"After breakfast, tell Albert he can lay up for the rest of the day, but he's gone tomorrow by noon. He's done around here."

"Wait a minute," Hurley growled. "I'll get him."

"Don't bother—I don't want him. He doesn't pull his weight."

"Well, if ya don't want him, ya don't want me either."

"As a matter of fact, Hurley, that would suit me just fine if you joined him."

"Hold on, now—"

"No, I mean it. I want both of you out of here—you sour up the place. Finish your coffee and pack up. Frank will unlock the shed for what you stored in there. See me for your week's pay."

Hurley glared at Roy.

"It's not a healthy thing yer doing, Mr. Big Boss Man."

"This is not the first camp I've ever run, and you're not the first tough man that's ever worked for me. I've been through all this before. There's nothing new or scary about you."

Roy pushed back his chair. He crossed one leg over the other which opened his coat just enough to reveal the heel of a pistol.

Hurley raised his coffee cup and poured the half filled contents splashing onto the table. He slammed the overturned tin cup into the middle of the puddle.

"I reckon I'm finished with my coffee." He rose and left the table, giving the bench a jarring kick with his massive shoe.

"Frank, go on and keep an eye on them until they leave. Put this in your belt so they can see it."

He removed the gun from the shoulder holster, spun it and placed the handle in Frank's hand.

Frank followed the irate man, positioning the gun under his belt.

"Warren," Roy called.

WC leaned over his plate and looked past the men in between.

"Sir?"

"Are you as good at hunting as you made yourself out to be?"

WC looked at his plate and put the tines of his fork into a puddle of gravy. "I don't brag, sir."

Pokey, who sat at the middle of the table, let biscuit crumbs drop from his lips as he spoke. "Does that mean there ain't nothing to brag about?"

"It means talking don't prove anything. But if you want meat send me out to hunt. I know how to find game, and I hit what I aim at." He wiped a path of biscuit through the gravy and placed it into his mouth.

Another man laughed. "And he don't brag."

Pokey began pleading. "Send me out hunting, Roy. I'd for sure fill Cookie's skillet."

"Seen you shoot, Pokey," the man next to him laughed. "You'd need a shotgun to hit a tree. And even then you'd be better off to close your eyes."

"Aw, shut up, Bob. C'mon, Roy, let me hunt."

"I don't believe I will. You're dangerous enough with a saw; I can't imagine what you'd be like with a gun in your hands. Warren, we'll get your gun from the tool shed after breakfast. You sure that small caliber 22 will do the job. You want a shot gun?"

"No sir. My gun will be fine. It shoots straight and doesn't make much noise, like a shot gun."

"Don't fail us. I don't want to have to put Pokey in Cookie's apron."

"I can cook," Pokey insisted, while the men all groaned. "Give me a little beef, some onions, and them little fire peppers and I'll make you a hash you'll dream about the rest of your lives."

Cookie marched down to WC tying the apron strings around his waist. "Now, don't shoot up the meat. We don't want blood all over the good parts."

"Do you cook the head?"

"Do I what? 'Cook the head'? No, I don't cook the head."

"Won't any meat be wasted then." He rose to leave.

Pokey called out, "You reckon I ought to come with you?"

WC stopped and rested his hand on the door casing. He turned back, grinning shyly. It was the first time the men had seen anything like it on his face.

"Well, yeah, Pokey, I could use you if you could be spared."

"Well, all right, boy! How about it, Roy?"

WC smiled fully.

"Yes, sir, Mr. Roy, how about it? I believe I'll need someone to haul the game for me."

Pokey laughed and threw his spoon. WC ducked and it hit the wall, leaving a mark of breakfast. The boy wagged his butt. About a dozen spoons flew at him. He ran out laughing.

* * * * *

He walked the road east, following the line of woods several miles away from the noise of the camp. Hunting would be better; the game would not be so cautious or scarce. The land rolled up from a river. The woods and meadow edges were perfect. He stepped inside the woods and began kicking brush piles. At the edge he knew he would find rabbits, their meat tender and sweet from the nearby grasses. It was easy hunting. In no time, he had picked off four. Three head shots, one in the neck—it hopped when it should have stayed still. He held each limp animal reverently. To him they were such funny soft creatures, quiet and scared. He cut the tendon in their hind legs, ran twine through the holes and tied them around his waist. Their bodies slung off his hips like furry holsters.

He shot one more rabbit and then entered the woods to hunt squirrels. He stopped briefly at a small clear running creek, scooped a hand full of water, rinsed his mouth and then continued on, listening for chatter, stalking from tree to tree.

The first squirrel sat in a patch of light on a mossy log. It pawed a nut around in its teeth. A second squirrel, high up and trees away, cussed it out, poised threateningly on the trunk. WC hid behind a tree, able to see both of them. The trick here was to bag both animals, and that depended on determining which one to shoot first. He thought, "Squirrels on the ground are in more danger; they'll hide and not come out. Ones in a tree are cocky, safe feeling and curious."

He kept his eyes on the busy, alert little animals and put a second bullet between his teeth, brassy-tasting. They had no idea he cocked the firing pin back and lifted the rifle. The one on the log held the nut in its mouth and scratched its shoulder with a hind leg. WC exhaled and put soft pressure on the trigger. The rifle cracked and echoed off the trees around him. The squirrel tumbled from the log, pitching the nut into the air. It landed in a bed of leaves; its forelegs prayed under its chin.

After firing, WC immediately ejected the spent shell and loaded the cartridge from his mouth. He watched the second squirrel. It pressed against the trunk, searching the area for the alien sound. Caution, finally sent it scampering to the back of the tree, out of WC's view.

He sighted at the crotch of an upper limb, expecting the animal to show. Sure enough, more curious than careful, it hunched its head and shoulders out to locate the danger.

"Crack!"

The squirrel fell. Its little claws pulling small pieces of bark through the air. He reloaded and waited for others to arrive and perhaps show themselves. But nothing stirred, except crows angling over the tree tops above him.

He moved from hiding, collected the warm bodies and added them to his waist. Paid to hunt. It was the easiest, most enjoyable money he would ever make.

He began stalking further east, quartering to the south, deeper into the unfamiliar woods. Every so often, he would mark his trail with a broken branch, scuffed moss, or an upturned twig stabbed into the earth. He would not be able to live it down if he were to get lost and have to be rescued by Pokey. Imagine the jokes they would make at his expense, and never send him out again.

He stalked on, watching the trees, listening. There were animals of one kind or another all around him. They were at home—in their kitchen. As a stranger, the only advantage he had was being quiet, unseen, and unexpected. He hoped they would just carry on with their business. When they do, they make a fuss. All living things do—scrambling for food, for territory, for dominance, for survival.

He heard leaves rustling ahead of him. He knelt on one knee behind a tree. Something was scratching in the leaves beyond the standing oaks running into a swale and past the dead tree that lay rotting into the earth. Whatever made the noise WC could not see it.

A squirrel began barking from high in a tree.

"And you hear it, too," WC said to himself. "Can you see it?"

The leaves were dug at powerfully again. WC saw where the sound came from, across the swale from behind the fallen oak, but it was screened by branches and bushes. He sat still, waiting to identify the animal making such a racket.

The squirrel had stopped barking, but then started again. It had jumped trees, and WC took a moment to relocate it. The little animal was not happy with whatever was below. It directed its disgust exactly where WC could hear the sound. Whatever was digging in the leaves and twigs was no friend of Mr. Squirrel.

The hunter had to be patient. Relax, and let the prey be at home. WC began counting, slowly. The animal would eventually move.

He reached one-hundred and had not heard a repeat of the sound. The squirrel had moved and WC lost it. He found it again in a tree closer. It sat on its hunches, flicking its tail out of an "S" curve, and scolded the animal below that had also moved—noiselessly. It had snuck closer to WC, but he still could not make it out.

Movement behind some brush caught his eyes. He could not see anything definite. It blended into the background, making it almost invisible—like spots on spots.

Just when he thought he had lost it, the thing moved again. He raised the rifle and aimed at the center of the massive movement.

"What in Sam Hill is that thing?" He raised his eyes over the sights to get a better look.

It moved again, and he beheld the biggest bird he had ever seen. What kind could be that big? It was not a buzzard and no chicken stood that upright.

The thing gobbled. He had never heard the sound before, but he knew it from books at school and the kids imitating it. It was a turkey. The only other one he had seen was headless and naked, lying in a roasting pan, smelling of sage and cornbread dressing.

The squirrel leaped to another tree and began chattering off behind WC's shoulder. The turkey was moving closer, off to his right and he followed it with the sights of the rifle. It would stop to dig, peck at the ground, survey the woods and move.

Where was he supposed to shoot? That tiny head? It would be some shot if he could do it, but what if he missed? Do they fly? Would he have time for a second shot? A sure shot at the center would ruin meat.

"Come closer and shoot for the head," he resolved.

"But it's so restless," doubt fought back. "Will it ever stand still? And there's that squirrel I don't want to miss."

For some reason known only to nature itself, the turkey began angling away. It was now as close as it was going to get. WC sighted on its eye, but looked up, uncertain of himself. He did not want to miss, so he lowered the aim to the chest.

"Dang it, dang it, dang it!" he berated his lack of confidence. He raised the sight up the neck and leveled it on the head.

"If I miss, it'll run or fly and be gone. But so what?"

He rested his finger against the trigger.

"Sure would like to carry this bird out with me. Hold still, Mr. Bird, hold still."

"Crack!"

The bird leaped into the air and fell heavily to the ground.

"One down."

He turned his attention to the squirrel and caught sight of it scuttling to the backside of a large bough—only its ears and eyes showing. It was plain enough to see, but not enough at which to aim. WC walked closer and the squirrel lifted enough to keep him in sight. Still not a good target.

WC remembered a time he had been hunting with his daddy and been told about the time his grandfather had "barked" a squirrel. Actually shot bark off a limb, knocking a squirrel out of a tree. He had not believed it, but Della had confirmed the fact saying, "There wasn't a bullet hole or blood anywhere on that animal—just a broken neck."

WC looked at the limb just above his squirrel. Scaly bark curled off it.

"If it can be done once, I don't see why it can't be done again."

If he could hit that one hunk of bark the right way, it should smack that squirrel on top of its head. He aimed at several spots before deciding and firing. The bullet thunked into the limb. It was aimed too low to chip it away. The squirrel raised and hunched back down.

"Teasing me? I don't mind, as long as you give me a second chance." He stepped further away and aimed again.

"Crack!"

The hunk disappeared, but so did the eyes and ears. Nothing had fallen. It must have run off on the back side of the tree. WC watched for it to reappear somewhere else. It did not.

He looked back at the bough and saw a tail slowly descending. Then the hind legs swung into view. He walked beneath the tree and saw the squirrel's front paws dug into the bark. One paw let go and it hung cock-eyed and swinging. It could not last much longer. The other paw dragged loose, and the unconscious animal dropped through the leaves, glancing off branches. WC had to step out of the way it landed so close. He twisted its neck and looped it under the twine. Now, for sure, he knew granddaddy barked that squirrel.

The turkey was sprawled in the leaves. WC pulled a wing open and spread its tail feathers. It was beautiful—layered with close brown colors, edged and daubed in black, creating patterns that ruffled and striped its appearance.

"And men and women in Little Rock think they get dressed up. You must have been able to put on a show, all right. Not much to say for your head though."

He squeezed the carcass to see if it was solid or all fluff.

"How am I going to carry you? Must weigh over twenty pounds. I wish, now, Roy would have let Pokey come along."

He recalled his jesting and smiled. The thought of providing a turkey meal to the camp thrilled him.

He broke a sturdy branch off a tree, cut it shoulder-width wide and tied the huge wings over it. After knotting a short length of twine to each end of the branch, he sat in front of the turkey and pulled the strings, one at a time, over his shoulders and tied each one separately to a strap of his overalls. It felt balanced when he stood, but too low. He sat to take the bird's weight off and retied the strings to pull the turkey higher on his back. It felt better, but sure did tug his overalls.

"What must I look like from behind?"

His whole backside was covered with feathers and fur—turkey wings set for flight, clutching five rabbits and three squirrels.

CHAPTER FOURTEEN

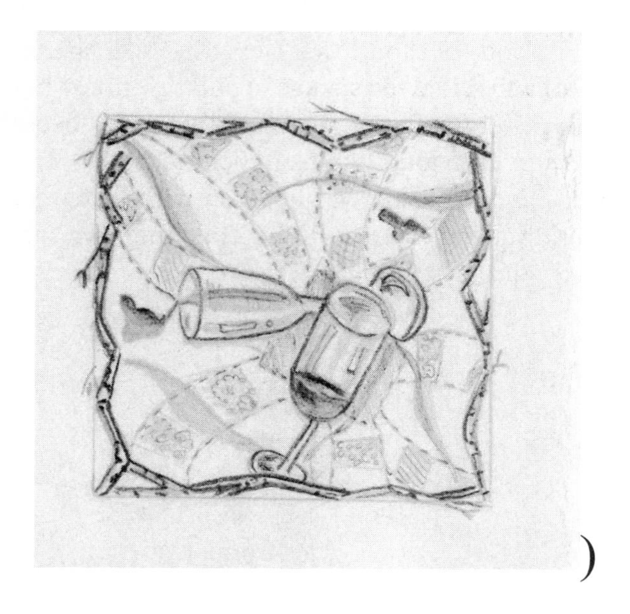

)

THE PICNIC

That lifeless old bird had to weigh a million pounds the way the twine cut into his shoulders and hoisted the overalls into his crotch. He had not realized he had hunted so deeply into the woods. It was a long way back to the road and he was happy to find the banks of the little creek again. It felt good to drop everything to the ground and rest in the shallow water and cool down. The edge of the woods was not far off; a wall of sunlight ascended through the trees ahead. It had to be shortly after noon.

He splashed a final handful of water on his face and wet his hair. The belt of fat stiffened rabbits seemed to be heavier than when he had loosened it. He tied the turkey as high on his back as he could and looped the squirrels under the twine.

Shouts rolled faintly down the creek bed. WC instinctively crouched. The voices were angry—someone was cursing. He did not have to worry, though. They were not near enough to concern him, so he started for the daylight.

He walked out of the woods, crossed the grassy field and stepped into the road. He trudged ahead. Camp had to be about two miles up the road, he thought. None of the men would be expecting a turkey. Cookie was going to split with surprise. He felt embarrassed thinking of the attention he would be receiving.

The road rose slightly before him and he leaned into it. He was grateful when it dipped, until he saw a one horse carriage drawn up beside a huge oak tree. The tree provided shade in a field of Queen Anne's lace, nodding on the slope toward the woods and the little creek running just inside.

"The rig must belong to the voices I heard," he thought. "It's lucky whoever owns it. It's a nice one. And that horse's shiny black coat is so slick, dust wouldn't settle on it. Pampered thing wouldn't know a plow from a porch swing."

Someone was having a picnic. Beneath the tree a large quilt was spread. He recognized it as the wedding ring quilt because of the interlocking rings designed throughout the white space. But as he drew closer, something was wrong.

The picnic basket was beside the road, turned over, and caved in—like someone had kicked it. On the quilt, a china plate was tipped over and half a sandwich strewn out, its contents soiling across the field of white. Two wine glasses lay nearly drained and staining blood-red through a set of rings, and the wine bottle stood tilted off in the grass.

A man in a white suit laid face down beside the mess, one foot twisted awkwardly in a second plate. A flat straw hat tipped like a mushroom from an overturned glass salt shaker. It seemed to grow just out of the man's reach. It did not look right to WC. The scene was too empty—too disorderly for all the intention. He debated whether he had any business at that quilt, especially covered in dead animals.

"Mister?" He called. There was no response. WC picked up the basket and took a step off the road, into the shade.

"Mister? Is this your basket?"

A woman's faint scream froze him. It came from the woods, but a man's angry bark cut the sound short.

WC looked at the man on the ground—he never moved. He let go of the basket and drew closer. Patterns of sunflowers stitched amongst the wedding rings came into view, and the silverware was embossed with roses.

"Mister, you all right? That your woman back in the woods?"

His pockets were turned inside out. WC walked to the far side of the quilt.

"Beg your pardon, sir—"

The man's eyes were wide open and stared blankly along the rumpled cloth at a sliced tomato. A swollen knob raised on his forehead oozed blood.

"Oh, my Lord."

WC circled back and tapped the man's leg.

"Can you wake up, mister?"

He rolled him to his back. The man's eyes never moved and his arm flopped over striking the earth lifelessly.

"Lord God, Almighty, he's dead."

A scream from the woods again chilled him. He scanned the road, but it was empty. No one was coming. The distance to camp was too far, close to two miles.

Another scream and he turned back to the woods.

"Johnnn—" The cry was muffled and followed by cursing.

"What am I suppose to do?" WC asked. "Someone's got a woman in there and killed this man."

He hoped someone else had heard, but the road, the horizon, was empty. No one else was coming. He was the only one.

"I must be crazy. What could I do?"

He fumbled at the strings holding the carcasses on his body, untied them, left them in a heap beside the man, and sprinted down the slope in the direction of the cries. Before entering the woods he jumped a lady's straw hat. Its yellow ribbon had been mashed by a dirty heel print.

If he continued at his reckless speed he was going to give himself away. He slowed down. Whoever had the woman took no effort to cover their tracks and was far enough ahead so WC could move quickly. Once he caught up, he would have to be much more deliberate. And what then?

His heart raced, his breath was short, though he had not run that far or that hard. He had to stop and rest; pulling the bolt back on the chamber to reassure himself the rifle was properly loaded. When he had recovered he wiped the mustache of sweat from his lip and followed the shuffled leaves.

WC rose out of a ravine and heard voices. He dropped to a knee, but was unable to see anything through the trees. Crouching low, he grew more cautious, but kept a steady pace to close the distance.

"Whoever killed that man and took the woman wouldn't be too worried about breaking a skinny kid's neck, if he got hold of it. I have to catch up, get them in sight, so I see them before they see me."

Something flickered between trees just ahead. He froze. He had gotten closer than he expected. He lowered himself slowly to the ground, slipped the rifle through the bib of his overalls and crawled behind a tree. He sat against its gnarly bark, panting.

"Did they see me? That's just what I was afraid might happen. What in the world am I doing? Lord, I wish daddy were here."

He peered around the tree, saw nothing, but heard the trudging of feet against the forest floor.

"I've almost caught up—what now?"

The woman's voice cried out and a man cursed her. WC crawled away from the tree, and forward to a bush, a log, and then another tree.

An argument broke out—two voices assaulting each other.

"Hold under her knees. I'm carrying all the weight, ya half-wit."

"Watch who yer calling a 'half-wit.' "

"Up higher! Higher! She's not a wheelbarrow, ya know."

"Quit yer kicking, girl. Hit her for me."

"How am I supposed to do that? My hands are full."

"Just a minute. Hang on tight to her."

WC heard something impacted and a brief squeal.

"There. Now I got her better. Let's go." The leaves scuffled.

WC pictured the scene: two men, desperate with a dead man's weight on their backs, carrying a woman between them. Two of them and only one of him. He scurried on, listening to their voices, but still unable to see them.

He was in the open, crossing between two distant trees, when they came into view—two hundred feet ahead. WC was completely exposed. All they had to do was look up and he would be seen. Inch by inch, imperceptibly, he stooped, and then pressed himself flat to the ground. He watched as the men carried a woman in a fancy city dress. She was limp, her arms and body swinging between them.

WC crawled to a tree. He could not lose sight of them—no more surprises. He stole from tree to tree; careful to cover his movement by obstructions between him and the men he was closing on. Each stealthy creep or quick dart to the next tree brought him closer, as the men seemed to be tiring and slowing.

He had gained enough to see them clearly. The girl was unconscious. The man at her shoulders had a beard and moustache—it was Hurley. All he could see of the other man was his back and the shotgun slung across it, but it was definitely Albert. There was the same balding head, and the skinny frame struggled with his share of the load.

"I tell ya, if them clothes were off she'd weigh forty pounds lighter."

"We're not stopping for any of that yet. If ya had left her alone, like I told ya, she'd be walking. But no, ya had to paw at her—turn her into a wildcat. Ya got to listen to what I tell ya."

"I do."

"No, ya don't. Did ya pull him into the weeds? No, ya left him out in the open. Ya went through his pockets, and then lost yer head and commenced getting the girl all riled up."

"Well, she's heavy and I'm about to give out."

"We're not stopping until we get to the river."

As they began to slip out of view WC kept pace with them.

"They're running for the river. Maybe I should circle in front and cut them off? What would I do—kill them? My Lord!"

He put that thought out of his mind. But what other choices would there be against two grown men? Wounding them would be no good. Bullets from a twenty-two would not even slow them down, if they came after him. All he could do was keep following, and hope for something good to happen.

The men flushed a bird, sending it straight toward WC. It saw him, veered sharply away, its wings becoming clamorous, and made for the tree tops. WC sank to his knees and held his breath.

"Hold on. Put her down," Hurley ordered.

"Why? What's wrong?"

"I said, 'put her down!' "

The woods became silent. WC gained a deep appreciation for hunted squirrels. He wanted to crane his neck around the massive tree that screened him from the men's view. He knew better. Heightened caution was safest—and listening—listening for any movement in his direction.

"There ain't nothing out there."

"Shut up!"

WC ached to know what was happening on the other side of the tree, but held himself hidden—alert. He planned escape lanes if one of them decided to backtrack his way. Finally, he heard movement and the unmistakable exhaling of someone sitting down.

"Throw me the bottle. I want a drink."

"Now yer talking."

WC heard the bottle snatched out of the air. He crawled directly to the tree and laid flat behind its roots, watching as they drank. Hurley tipped the bottle up for a swallow, tossed it to Albert and took several steps in WC's direction, scanning the woods.

"That man was a surprise—never figured him to fight back, try to wrestle yer shotgun away. Showing off for the woman."

"Yeah. And what about me? 'Eat ya some gun stock, feller.' Pnnnkk! He must have been some tender mama's boy, to let that little ol' tap git the best of him. Pnnnkk! Dropped him dead as taters."

He tipped the bottle for a second drink.

"Ya chunked that city boy a good one, all right. Didn't know ya had it in ya."

"I didn't mean to kill him. His own fault for being soft-headed."

"With him laid out like that, he'll be easy found and people on our trail." Hurley took the offered bottle and swigged from it.

"The girl's real pretty, ain't she, Hurley?"

"Never mind. Let's git going."

WC watched them carry her off again.

"Once they get to the river and into the bayou no one will track them." They disappeared behind a tree and WC crept after them.

They had not traveled far before Albert complained again about needing to rest. He whined and pleaded until they stopped.

"She's dressed real fine, ain't she?"

"Don't worry, we'll get to that. Check that wallet."

Albert pulled a wallet from his pocket and thumbed the bills inside.

"Whoo-eee! There's maybe forty, fifty dollars. Thank ya very much, Mr. Fancy Pants."

"Let me have that." Hurley counted the money. "There's seventy-seven, and I'll keep it for now." He pulled his coat open and pocketed the wallet inside.

"Seventy dollars! C'mon, I done carried it this far—let me hang on to it."

"Git yer hands off my coat." He shoved Albert stumbling away and grabbed his partner's neck with one hand.

"Ya'll git yer share at the house. But right now, all I need ya to do is pick her up."

"Okay, okay, quit choking."

"Don't pester me about it."

"I won't."

Hurley threw him to the ground.

"Now forget the money and let's go."

Albert massaged his neck before moving to the woman.

"When we gonna have our fun with her?"

"She won't be going past the river."

They started off again. The way Albert wheezed and floundered with her weight, WC was afraid the lady might not make it that far.

They argued and cussed each other—Albert wasting his precious breath on idle threats. He kept suggesting they rest, but Hurley ordered him to keep moving.

WC came to a long opening. To cross it, he would chance the possibility of being seen and coming as close as he dared; to skirt around, he would lose sight of them and fall too far behind. He waited and watched the men leave the clearing and plunge into the stand of trees.

"I'll cross. Stay low and go slow."

He crawled on hands and knees, watching them appear and disappear through the trees and brush. With one final scramble he reached a tree and sat to catch his breath.

"How much longer? How's it going to end?"

He leaned around the tree to locate them and once again stalked their trail.

The girl regained consciousness—WC could hear her crying.

"Aw, dry up, unless ya want me to hit ya again."

She begged them not to hurt her. Albert threatened to put a knife in her and she was quiet.

Albert's legs finally crumpled, sitting him down with the girl's head and shoulders in his lap. He was out of breath.

"I can't... make... another step."

"Ya empty-headed crybaby. I'd have done better with one of yer young 'uns." Hurley dropped the lower half of the girl's body.

She squealed and covered her face with her hands.

"C'mon, Hurley... It ain't but a quick run to the river from here. Nobody's catching up with us—we're clean away, for sure. I don't want to put the fun off anymore."

The girl cried out and tried to roll away, but Albert held her fast, wrapping his arms and legs around her.

"Gotcha, sweetheart. Locked in my arms."

Hurley squatted in front of her.

"What's yer name?"

The girl turned away and ducked her head.

"I said, 'What's yer name?'" He took a handful of hair and yanked her back to him. She screamed.

"Yer name?"

"Virginia. Please."

"Please what?" Albert put his lips to her ear. "Please love me?"

"Don't hurt me."

Albert laughed and then kissed her.

She cried and moaned, "No."

"Yer sweet, girl."

"Git back, Albert."

"She's got the sweetest mouth ya'd ever want to taste. Go on, take a turn." He jumped up, unslinging his shotgun and leaned it against a log.

Virginia scooted away from Hurley. He grabbed her ankle and dragged her back to him. He rammed two fingers under the collar of her blouse and gave a vicious jerk. Buttons popped away and scattered to the ground—some dangled from ripped fabric. He gave another tear and held a tattered portion of the blouse above his head. Albert knelt beside him and took it.

The girl was helpless against Hurley's power. She kicked and struck at him, but he continued to bore in and tear at her.

"Lord God, Almighty." WC could not believe what he was seeing. The man had to be stopped.

He pressed the rifle to his shoulder—the front sight bisecting the back of Hurley's head. The woods reverberated with the girl's screams and the man's growling assault. His head was right there—close as a squirrel's, bigger than a squirrel's, but it wasn't a squirrel's.

"My Lord, I can't shoot a man in the head." He lowered the rifle, tried to think, but the frightful screams and the horror of the scene staggered his mind.

Albert cheered as a handful of white scraps was thrown aside.

WC aimed again. They were hogs. Ugly mean beasts with not a thought for others. They didn't deserve to hurt that lady. He squeezed the trigger.

Nothing happened. No report, no man pitching forward. He looked at the rifle.

"What's wrong?" Nothing he could see.

He raised the gun, aimed and squeezed again, but it would not move. It felt locked. Locked! He had not cocked the pin back.

"Oh, God, Daddy! That man would be dead right now—with my bullet in his head. Oh, Daddy, I would have killed him."

Panic began ebbing away, replaced with calm. He knew what to do now as he held a second bullet between his teeth and moved behind a bigger tree to cover his entire body. He pulled the knob of the firing pin back and aimed around the edge of the tree. As loudly as he could, he yelled.

"Daddy, I found them!"

He fired the rifle at the shotgun. The stock and barrel separated and tumbled in two pieces to the ground.

"I broke their gun," he hollered.

The woods were stunned into silence. Both men twisted around to find the voice. Trees were all they saw.

"Hurry! Uncle Otis, down here. Get the others." He fired the second bullet into the air.

"There's two of them and she's with them." He ripped another shot into the leaves above the men. They ducked and began running away—jumping deadfalls and slapping branches.

"They're getting away. Hurry! Bring up the dogs, Mr. Bell."

WC stood. They had disappeared and he could hear their crashing fade farther into the echoing woods. He ran to the lady.

Virginia moaned and clutched jagged rags of her petticoat to her bosom. He knelt beside her, murmuring.

"They're gone, ma'am. No one's here to hurt you anymore. It's all right." He patted and stroked her arm.

"Those men are running off, but we best be leaving. They might decide to come back. C'mon, stand up and let's go."

He helped her sit up, but there was so little to cover herself with she refused to move further.

"No, I can't. You and your father would see me."

"My daddy isn't coming. Or my uncle. It's only me, ma'am. We have to get away from here, right now. Please, I don't mean to shame you, but–" He grabbed the hem of her skirt and pulled it up to her hands.

"Cover up with this. Now, put your arm around my neck and I'll help you stand."

"I hurt all over."

"Yes, ma'am, they were rough with you."

She leaned on him, limping and whimpering.

"John. Where's John?"

"He's back at the rig." That was all he thought right to tell her.

He led her out of the woods above the picnic quilt in order to avoid John's sprawled body. He rested her beside the road while he ran for the horse and buggy and drove it back.

She had not moved, but sat huddled into her skirt. He took leaves from her hair and then helped her into the seat.

"Isn't John with you? Is he all right?"

"No ma'am. He's not."

She raised her hand and showed him a ring sparkling there.

"He proposed marriage to me. We're engaged."

CHAPTER FIFTEEN

THE JAIL

WC and Cookie laid Virginia on one of the bunks. Cookie tended her while WC ran to the woods to find Roy. The entire crew was called in and sent on errands in every direction. WC was told to go home; Pokey would drive him. He did not like the idea.

"If it's lost wage worrying you, kid, the company's going to take care of that. You do what I tell you."

Roy held his shoulders and bent down to him.

"Maybe you haven't gotten it yet. You're a danged hero—you saved that woman's life. And that's enough for anyone to do in one day. Now get in the wagon."

"When do you want me back?"

"If no one sends for you by Sunday, be back for work Monday morning."

"Mr. Roy?"

"Can't you just get on that wagon? What is it?"

"There's a shotgun they left in the woods. It's in two pieces, close to where they'll find the rags of that woman's dress."

"Good. I'm glad you told me."

"And all the game I hunted is by the quilt."

"We'll take care of it. We'll take care of everything. Haul him out of here, Pokey. Get him home."

* * * * *

Dedge came plugging to the porch as WC finished telling his story to Della.

"Get yerself fired, did ya?" He dropped into the porch chair and laughed.

"No, I didn't get fired. They closed the camp down."

Della took up the story.

"One of the workmen drove him home, and now WC's been telling me a man was killed by two men from that camp and he kept them from killing a woman too. Lord, how did you do that?"

"There's not much to say about it. Just that when I came up on them they turned her loose and I brought her out."

"But how did it happen? What did you do?"

"Don't waste yer breath, Della," Dedge scoffed. "We'll have to get the truth from somewhere else anyway."

* * * * *

The next afternoon, Jacob Binsley, the Constable, questioned WC, probing him for details and writing the boy's story in a notebook. They walked back to the porch and Jacob reported to Della and Dedge the progress of the hunt for the killers.

"The dogs lost their trail. They whipped off southeast, toward Little Rock. The sheriff and some men are in Hickory Plains waiting if they double back for Albert's home. They must be wetter than catfish, as much time as they've spent in the water. We'll find them."

"Is WC in any danger?"

"I don't believe so, Della. From his story, they don't know it was him that scared them off. Besides, they're too worried about their own skins to come after his."

"That woman back up everything this boy's told?" demanded Dedge.

"Well, she's in shock. No one's pressing her on it right now."

"Yeah, just as I thought. It's only his story we're hearing."

"She's in pretty bad shape, but I want to tell you, she keeps asking about 'John' and wanting to see 'that little boy from the woods.' From what he's told us, we ain't got any reason to doubt him a bit." He turned to WC and pointed the notebook at him.

"One thing I want to know is why you didn't shoot them?"

WC shrugged.

"I don't know. Just didn't want to kill anybody."

Jacob nodded his head.

"They didn't seem to mind, though, did they?"

"No, sir. Pleased themselves was all."

The only other interest WC had that day was to ask about Tommy Irene. Della told him Clair still had not let her go. There was such need of her. He decided it was time someone else knew about the trouble Dar Davis was causing. After church, he would give Tommy a choice: tell someone herself, or he would do it.

* * * * *

Brother Ramsey stormed along in his sermon. The sun had not yet broke over the trees shading the small group's gathering in the outdoor sanctuary, but with his strenuous style the man was already drenched from the Spirit. He folded his suit coat precisely and laid it aside on a chair. It did not distract him or alter the cadence of his preaching. The white handkerchief, aloft from his upraised hand, had mopped all the sweat it could endure, and joined its companion already draped from the edge of the pulpit: twin testimonies of his convictions.

WC knew the collar had to be unbuttoned and the tie removed before anyone could even begin to think of the sermon's end.

"I'll read it again." Brother Ramsey made one of his infrequent stops behind the pulpit, bent to the Bible and read.

" 'Their feet run to evil, they make haste to shed innocent blood.' "

He paused, holding a finger in his place in the book, and looked at the congregation before continuing.

" 'Their thoughts—' "

He stepped back, gazing out at the people. He loosened his tie, unbuttoned his collar and repeated in an intense whisper.

" 'Their thoughts…' "

The words were lifted and held lightly as a cloud for all to consider. He leaned back to the book.

" 'Their thoughts are thoughts of iniquity; wasting and destruction are in their path.' "

The tie came off and he brought the passage to life with renewed energy—overflowing with examples of "wicked thinking."

The "shedding of innocent blood" was already on everyone's mind and the preacher made the Lord's best use of it. A third handkerchief sought the sweat from his forehead. He turned the Bible back a page and held out his arms. In an exhausted and hoarse voice he pleaded.

> “ ‘Let the wicked forsake his way, and the unrighteous man his thoughts; and let him return unto the Lord, and he will have mercy upon him: and to our God, for he will abundantly pardon.’ ”

WC thought the Lord mighty generous to do such a thing and doubted he could ever be as merciful.

Della nudged WC and then turned toward the aisle. Jacob Binsley stood there motioning for them to join him at the rear. She took WC’s arm and they slid off the bench. Eyes roved from the preacher to follow them. Whispers were passed.

Brother Ramsey broke into his nearly completed sermon.

“Jacob. Do you have an announcement you wish to make?”

“Preacher, I’m sorry to disturb your service—I am. The Little Rock police have two men in custody—caught them in the River Rat Shacks at the waterfront. I’m escorting Della and WC to the city, so the boy can identify them.”

“You all go ahead. Take the brother to do the Lord’s work.”

“Amen,” everyone chorused and turned to see Della and WC directed to a carriage drawn by two horses.

WC thought his own work was quite enough. The preacher didn’t need to be laying work from the Lord on him too.

Tommy Irene waved when he looked back, but he was unable to wave in return as Jacob guided him toward the carriage. He had just missed forcing her to relieve him of his promise. He had missed by the preacher's winding down and the verses of an altar call.

* * * * *

Jacob drove the horses hard, and it was not long before they passed the logging camp and approached the picnic site. WC saw how the grass and Queen Anne's lace had all been trampled by men and dogs. He did not say a word to his mother.

Jacob slowed and pointed the place out to her. She turned to watch the area pass, imagining the horror her son must have witnessed. Her eyes met WC's, but he looked away.

A uniformed policeman met them just outside the city, and they were transferred into an open car and driven by back streets toward the jail. The policeman had only a few words for them.

"The whole city is turned out at the station. Captain Barnston doesn't want you to have to part the seas to get in the door. We're going in through the back."

They turned into an alley. A man pacing at the corner held his hat and ran after the car, shouting question after question. Della turned to see what all the yelling was about.

"He's a newspaper man. Every paper in the state has got someone here to interview Warren."

"I don't want any newspapers."

"That's why we're going around back."

At the station, a sergeant opened a back door and hurried Della and WC inside. The news man cursed as the door was closed and locked in his face.

"We don't need any company," he said. "Wait here. I'll let the captain know you've arrived."

They stood in an empty room. Della stared straight ahead; WC looked at the floor around his shoes. They heard voices and scuffling behind the other two doors, but it was none of their business and they kept their attention on what was ahead.

Bill Barnston entered the room. He introduced himself to Della and shook WC's hand so hard it hurt.

"That's a fine young man you've got."

"I've reason to be proud of him. Besides what he did for that woman."

"Yes, ma'am, I've had the pleasure of seeing that myself." Barnston beamed at him. "You won't find any nonsense in him, will you?"

"There's not been much occasion for such. He could use some."

"Yes, ma'am, he deserves it."

WC knelt to one knee, untied and retied his shoe. Whatever he had to do, he wished they'd get on with it.

"Warren Carl, before we walk you through the jail, I've sent for someone to make you and your mother more comfortable here in the city."

He opened the door and Alma Shearcott marched in with her gloved hand extended toward Della. Behind her stood Mr. Shearcott and Lester O'Dell.

"You must be Warren Carl's mother. What a pleasure."

Alma took Della's hand, pressed it in both of hers and unexpectedly embraced the woman in her arms. WC saw his mother's startled hands tentatively rest on Alma's hips. Alma released her and stepped back. She dabbed her eyes with a lace handkerchief.

"Look at me—permitting my emotions to take such liberties." She wiped her eyes again.

"I'm Alma Shearcott. I cannot believe I was so forward." She laughed at herself. "Your son was our dinner guest, and a more charming one we've never had."

She introduced her husband and Lester and then moved to stand in front of WC. She restrained her hands from touching his face by finally clasping them together at her bosom. She just gazed at him.

"Mrs. Shearcott, how d'ya do?" He reached out a hand.

"I'm doing fine. Just fine, Warren Carl." They shook hands, keeping a distance.

"I'm pleased you got to meet my ma."

"Oh, I am, too. How are the both of you holding up?"

"I'd rather be at camp."

"Yes, I can imagine." She pulled Lester's arm and brought him beside her.

"Are you going to speak to your employee?"

He released her fingers from his sleeve.

"There's no need to yank me around, Alma." He looked back at her husband, who only shook his head and smiled. He straightened his lapels.

"Warren Carl, aren't we lucky to have such beautiful women to tell us what to do next." His hand extended from a white cuff.

"You told me I'd be proud to write that letter. And you were right. I'm thankful it was you there when the young woman needed help. You deserve all our gratitude."

"The turkey deserves that, sir."

Alma stepped in.

"Turkey? No one told me about a turkey."

"I shot it while hunting. It filled out what I needed to take back to camp and make Cookie happy. Without that bird, I'd have been another two, three hours picking off squirrels."

"Well then, we thank that turkey, too," Captain Barnston broke in. "I'm sorry to hurry you all along, but WC has an unpleasant duty to render to the state, and I'm sure he'd like to get it over with. Mrs. Dedge, would you be so kind as to accompany Alma and the men to my office? We'll be along in a few minutes."

"Just what will happen? Will my son be kept safe?" Her raised eyebrows challenged him to do anything less.

"He won't be in any danger. We have the men he saw: Hurleburt Sams and Albert Short. Sams still had Mr. Hempstill's wallet on him, if you can believe it. Said he found it. The other one's scared half to death and likely to confess anytime. I'll walk WC past the cells for a positive identification, and that'll be all we need for now."

"They can't harm him?"

"No, ma'am. There's no way they can get out."

She turned to Alma.

"I'm ready."

* * * * *

WC had never smelled anything as stale and repulsive as the cell area. It was dank, windowless and for someone accustomed to the open-air, the confines of mildew, close body odors and tobacco was sickening. The floor was solid cement, wet, and steel bars picketed both sides of the long passage. He counted ten electric lights dangling and glowing jaundice from the ceiling. Without a draft from open doors, without windows for the sun to stream, it seemed impossible that the sodden moldiness could truly dry out.

A policeman closed and locked the door behind them. He stood behind WC twisting a night stick in his hands.

"Everyone off your bunks and stand to the bars," he ordered. There were complaints, some shuffling of feet, and then fingers wrapped around the steel rods.

"Keep your hands on the bars and face forward."

Someone down the line mocked the words back.

Barnston looked down at WC and put his hand on his shoulder.

"Stay close to me. Look both sides and take your time. If you don't see them give me a tap and we'll move on. When you see them, remember the cell number."

They moved forward and stopped at the first set of cells. On one side a nearly clean shaven man in a suit smiled and shrugged. On the other side, two men with bruised and swollen faces stared through the bars.

Their skinned knuckles matched the bruises. The Chief felt a tap and moved ahead.

A man on the left said, "Ain't you a cute little feller."

The officer struck the bars and told him to shut up. WC tapped to go on.

A man farted, excused himself and then laughed. WC tapped again. And again. The inmates' clothes were twisted and wrinkled, their hair unkempt and faces grainy with whiskers. Everyone wore the same tired, slovenly expression.

Barnston repeated that he should take his time and be sure.

"Why did he say that?" WC wondered. "Had he missed them?"

Only three cells from the end. Maybe he had made a mistake. Maybe they really did not have the right men. Would he have to make this walk again? He was already nauseated.

In the upcoming set of cells WC saw a bald head pressed against the bars, the man's face hidden, ducked to the floor. His cell mate stared witheringly at him from behind a beard. It was Hurley.

The policeman banged his stick on the bars in front of Albert. "Eyes up, man. Get that head up."

Slowly, sadly, Albert lifted his head and recognized WC.

"Nooo. Not you."

"Shut yer mouth," Hurley growled.

WC tapped Barnston.

"Yer not the one that saw us," Albert moaned, rubbing the skin on his bald head.

"You ready to talk to us, Albert? I'll have this officer let you out of that cell if you want to tell me what happened."

Hurley warned Albert. "Don't ya say nothing."

"I don't know what happened, Mr. Barnston." He began weeping. "Ask the boy. Go ahead, son, tell him it wasn't us in them woods."

WC tapped harder—it hurt to watch.

"C'mon, ya know us. We worked together—please, don't give us away."

Hurley grabbed Albert by the throat.

"Keep quiet, ya gutless idiot!"

The policeman rammed the stick through the bars into Hurley's ribs, dropping him to the floor.

"Get me outta here," Albert shrieked. "He'll kill me. I didn't do nothing."

Hurley held his ribs and cussed Albert's outburst. He turned his eyes to WC.

"I'd have killed ya boy, if yer daddy hadn't been there."

WC yanked Barnston's coat, but the man stepped toward the cell.

"His daddy wasn't there. He ran you off by himself."

Hurley pulled himself up by the bars and sneered at WC.

"Yer skinny neck would break so easy." He limped away to lie on his bunk.

"Your neck will break before his ever will." The captain finally guided WC toward the door.

"Let's go. Don't worry, he isn't going anywhere."

Albert hollered after them as they reached the door.

"Help me, boy. I got a family—wife and four kids. I'm the man to them. It's hard. Ya don't know what it's like! Ya don't know what a man has to go through."

As the door unlocked and opened WC mumbled to himself.

"I reckon I know more about it than you think, mister."

"What's that you say, Warren?" Barnston asked.

"I have to get out of here."

As one door locked behind, another unlocked in front of them, and they entered a narrow hall that opened onto a room with people and police milling everywhere. WC leaned against the wall to quell the rising in his stomach and quiet the pounding in his head.

"You all right?"

"Just not sure if I'm coming or going. Can I rest a minute?"

"Take your time. I'm sorry to have kept you in there."

WC hung his head and swallowed back the saliva rushing into his mouth. He looked out into the room and saw a little boy's face, topped with flourishing, mussed up hair, on the opposite side of the desk sergeant's counter. The boy had pulled himself high enough to catch his chin on the edge and hold his head up. His eyes were fixed on WC.

"If you need the bathroom, it's behind this door here."

WC gave no answer; the boy's eyes held him so.

Barnston shook his shoulder. "Son?"

"Yes, sir?"

"I wondered if you wanted to wash up, or something?"

"No, sir. I washed in a tub last night. Wash every Saturday night for church."

"All right, let's go talk, and then we'll get your mother."

He trailed the captain behind the counter and approached the little boy. He piped out to WC.

"My daddy's back there."

WC halted across from him and looked into the boyish, tender face. It was smudged with dirt and could have been his own reflection several years ago.

"They got him locked up. Mama's come to see him."

A woman sitting in one of the chairs lined up against the wall told him to get down and hush. She held a baby, patting its back and rocking. In the chairs beside her sat two other children: a boy, probably the oldest, biting his finger nails, and a girl with her feet crossed and dangling toward the floor. Everyone's expression showed a glazing of undisturbed water over deep black mire.

The woman snapped, "Come and sit down, Lit'l Al. Leave that boy alone."

But he hung on and asked, "How old are ya? I'm gonna be five."

Barnston pulled at WC's sleeve, but he would not budge.

"I'm ten."

An unsuspected smack struck the boy and knocked him to the floor. His mother stood over him.

“I told ya to come and sit down.”

She returned to her chair without another word. The little boy rubbed his ear, shuffled to a wall and chair as far from her as he could get. He sat, drew his legs up into the seat, and put his head down. Maybe he cried then.

WC continued with Captain Barnston. Even with the boy’s voice echoing in his mind and the sympathy for what might happen to that family lined up against the wall, he did what he had to do—identified Albert and Hurley.

CHAPTER SIXTEEN

THE PORCH

The Shearcott's home rose three stories behind an ironwork fence. Two curving staircases ascended and met at a deep porch wrapped around three sides of the white exterior. Pecan trees shaded the south, and, like stately columns, seemed to bear the sky above the sun dazzled mansion. Alma had a luncheon served in the backyard garden and as she walked her guests out the towering double glass doors to the patio, Della halted, stunned by the magnificent sight of shrubs, flowers, ornamental trees, and rockwork landscaped throughout. Alma asked if anything was the matter.

"It's taken my breath. I never could imagine such a place."

She pulled WC to her side and whispered, "The Garden of Eden!"

They ate on bone china under a canopy of wisteria vine and were served cucumber chips in a dilled white sauce, sliced tomatoes sprinkled with fresh basil, and some kind of chilled fish. WC thought everything tasted flat and wished for something fried, but he politely finished his plate. Lavender was close by, reminding him of his mother's sachets.

He was asked if he preferred cantaloupe or freshly-turned ice cream for dessert. He answered by shrugging and saying he didn't care. Minutes later, a dish of melting scoops of ice cream piled into half a golden melon was placed before him.

He pulled his mother and whispered, "The Garden of Eden."

Despite the surroundings, the warm hospitality and the food, it was the most uncomfortable meal the two of them had ever eaten. They sat together, shoulder to shoulder, attending to the conversation and entering in whenever specifically addressed. Alma's love for conversing kept the conversation moving, though she did most of the talking while everyone else agreed.

Mr. O'Dell could not refrain from slapping WC on the back and referring to him as "My man." The boy felt out of place, constantly embarrassed, and longed to go home.

Mrs. O'Dell was the most beautiful woman WC had ever seen. Jocelyn's long brown hair was silky, wound up and bound with combs under a fluttering lacy hat. It amazed him that anyone could sit so straight. He liked that she was shy and rarely offered a word, except to answer a question. She smiled all the time, and WC was fascinated by her, probably in love, and stole glances whenever he could not be noticed.

Chief Barnston arrived as dessert dishes were being taken away. His presence, welcomed as it was, only stretched WC's dwindling patience to sit at a table for that length of time. It was pure misery to endure as the new guest was brought a plate of the lunch, and all sat while he ate and answered their questions about how the men were captured.

"They were gambling with some of the barge traffic men. My officers recognized them from Warren's description. There wasn't much to it—they're cowards when it comes to facing a man. Right, Warren? You ought to know."

WC shrugged and looked through the glass topped table at his mother's hands resting in her lap.

Barnston could not stay long and after finishing a cup of coffee, and waving away Alma's protests, he left.

Eddie Shearcott and Billy O'Dell were there too. Even with encouragement from their parents they chose to have little to do with WC. They nudged each other at the table, whispered sly jokes and purposely kept their distance. WC did not mind being uninvited as they ran into the house, but he hated the idea they might think he cared. All he wanted to do was go home.

Never, in all his life, had eating a meal been such drudgery. Della came to life, however, when the conversation turned to flowers. Shortly after, Alma suggested the women walk the garden. She admitted knowing little about gardening and left everything to her "horticulturalist." Della was intimately familiar with plants and eagerly identified flowers, pointed out groupings and stooped to inhale the fragrance of blooms. She communicated such an ardent relationship, both Alma and Jocelyn found touching and smelling irresistible themselves.

WC excused himself from the men and their talk of business and sat on a stone bench. He followed the progress of the women—one plain sparrow led between a bluebird and a yellow finch. The difference worried him—he was afraid for her feelings. But as they continued on their tour, Della began to laugh and even held Jocelyn's hand. With the garden only half explored, the three of them sat in the pavilion at the far end of the yard like sisters. WC couldn't believe it—Mrs. Shearcott was a magician with people.

Something thumped the ground close beside him. He looked down and saw a metal toy soldier. Another struck his leg. Eddie and Bill were shooting them out the second story window with a slingshot. They made grotesque faces at him, so he fired the two soldiers back at them. They ducked and raised their heads again, mocking. WC motioned for them to come down, but they disappeared.

Seeing just their heads above the window casement reminded him of Albert's little boy at the jail. It made him angry, considering the two pampered snobs in the house probably never gave a thought about their blessings. He could still hear that small voice and see those eyes.

"My daddy's back there... I'm gonna be five."

He felt guilty. Because of him those kids were losing their daddy. But it wasn't his fault, he told himself.

"I'm not to blame Albert is a killer. Are they better off now, even without someone to provide for them? What are they going to do?" He paced away from the house to think about it.

After a brief walk, he joined Mr. Shearcott and Mr. O'Dell at the flowing fish pond, where they stood smoking cigars.

"You think we'll get our women back?" Edward asked WC as he approached.

"Ma can keep you up all night talking flowers."

Lester pointed the ashy tip of his cigar at the pavilion.

"It appears they've struck a serious subject."

Alma and Jocelyn, on either side of Della, held her hands and listened intently as Della was speaking.

"I hate to interrupt the ladies, but Jocelyn and I have a musical function to attend this evening."

"Mr. O'Dell, before you go, might I ask a favor?"

"You don't want to take over my bank, do you?"

"No, sir, nothing like that."

"I was only joking. Go ahead and ask."

"Could some of my wage be split off, and sent someplace else.

Lester took a drag on the cigar and shook his head.

"It hasn't been done before. If someone wanted to allocate their money, they would be responsible for distributing it themselves."

"Why are you asking?" Edward wanted to know.

"I want part of my wage to go to Albert Short's wife to help with her kids. I don't know how to get it to her."

They knew nothing about the woman and the four children he had seen at the station, and promised to look into the matter immediately.

"What about my favor, sir? I can't carry the money to her every week."

"I promise she'll get help. Don't worry about it anymore."

* * ** *

The distance from Little Rock to home was amazingly short riding in a car. The officer drove into the yard, panicking and scattering the animals, except for Michael—he attacked the tires, flapped up to the hood and crowed until WC knocked him away. Della thanked the officer, and apologized for the mess their "ornery critter" deposited on the car.

He told them to think nothing of it.

"And the Chief wanted me to tell you that Albert confessed to everything, blaming the killing on his partner. Hurley went crazy when he heard about it. Tore up the cell, and four guards had to subdue him. I'll bet he's got a mighty big headache right about now." He touched his hat, nodded at Della and drove away.

Old Dedge ambled from the door and called out the only greeting he had for them.

"Ya going to fix me some supper, woman? I'm like to starve."

"You mean to say you can't fill your own plate with beans?"

WC went to the pig pen to look for Pee Wee. He wanted to hand feed him and enclose a small area in the barn for his safety. But he was not there. He was gone. WC found him hanging over a stall, above a slippery puddle of blood. Dedge wasn't about to make a meal of this pig—it was buried between two rows of corn, deep in the field.

* * * * *

Della brought WC a supper plate and sat with him in the barn while he ate.

"You going back to work in the morning?"

"I'm expected, yes."

"Why didn't you tell me what happened in the woods that day? Mrs. Shearcott told me—she got it from Mr. Barnston."

"Wasn't much to tell."

"Don't say that to me! Trailing those killers, shooting their gun apart, hollering like your daddy was there, that wasn't something to tell your mother? How do you think I feel being the last to know what you did—like I'm nothing? Like Custer on the porch: 'Ya gonna fix me some supper?' "

She turned from him.

“I don’t like being treated that way. Not one bit. Not by him anymore, and not by you. Things are going to change. I’m not putting up with it.”

“What do you mean?”

“I’ve as much right to my self as the rest of you. There are some things to think about, some choices to make, and I’m not saying a thing until I’ve got the broom all made to sweep out the house.”

“What choices? What broom? What are you talking about?”

“Won’t you be surprised.”

He followed her out of the barn and stood beside her as she sat on the mounting block by the door.

“It hurt my feelings, Son, being the last to know.”

“I’m sorry. I didn’t see it as anything to talk about.”

“Making those men think your daddy was there? How come you to think of that?”

“I almost killed a man, Ma. I pulled the trigger on him. The gun didn’t fire because I forgot to set the knob back… I didn’t want to kill anybody.”

“I’m glad you didn’t have to.”

“Daddy just came to me—I guess I prayed and called out to him.”

“And he was right there, wasn’t he?”

“I didn’t want to talk about it anymore than I had to. Someone might think I’m bragging.”

“Bragging? You think telling me what happened is bragging? I’m not asking you to do that. What I want is to listen to you. To hear you give a piece of yourself out and not hold so much back. My Lord, WC, keeping burdens to yourself will only—”

WC held up his hand to stop her.

"Listen." He began walking to the side of the barn.

"Sounds like someone shouting." Della followed him.

Tommy Irene was running through the potato field.

"Oh, Lord, what's happened, now?" Della ran to meet her.

"Aunt Della! Aunt Della!" She collapsed into her aunt's arms.

WC suspected the crisis, but she was safe with his mother now. He left them alone, feeling dread and shame, disappointed in himself.

"Why did I leave her on her own? What's so big about a promise now, if she's been hurt by that stupid Dar Davis? I should have told."

* * * * *

In the morning Tommy Irene remained in his mother's bed. Della walked WC to the bottom of the drive as he left for camp.

"Dar Davis was trying to carry on with her. He got what was coming to him—Clair caught him and clobbered him in the head with a shovel. Knocked him out. The boys thought it was funny, until she took the belt to them. Bill Philip ran off, but I guess she wore Jimmy out. Dar was lucky; he woke up and staggered off just before Block got home. Your uncle threw a fit, hollered at Irene, wanted to give her a licking, but Clair wouldn't allow it. He took off instead after Dar to kill him. Everything was in such an uproar, the poor thing run off and came to our place. I'll ride over later to see if she can stay a while. I'm sure it'll be all right."

WC listened with his head bowed.

"I believe you knew she was having trouble."

"Yes, ma'am, I did."

"That's why you pestered me to keep her."

"I promised her I wouldn't tell. I know I should have done different, but I couldn't believe the danger, until I saw those men with that woman. I was going to make Tommy tell or I would, but then we went to Little Rock. Right and wrong should be easy, but it's hard."

"That's sometimes the way of things."

"I couldn't make a choice. It was like putting on the only pair of shoes you got—good or bad.

"I know. It doesn't get any easier the older you get. I can testify to that. We do the best we can."

"I wish I would have done better."

"Don't we all, Son. Every day we're alive there's the chance to do better and be better. You have to change though, have higher hopes, and do things differently. I learned that from you. You don't have to give in to your troubles.

"You sound like Daddy now."

"I wouldn't mind that at all."

"Is Tommy Irene all right?"

"She's fine. The only hurt is shame. That's bad enough, I guess. She's one strong little girl. She bit that boy's lip—made him so mad he starting yelling and slapping her. That's when Clair came up on them."

"Is she mad at me?"

"Didn't say so."

“Tell her I said ‘Hi, and I’m sorry.’”

“I’ll do that. Don’t forget the get together at Uncle Otis’ on Saturday. I’ll carry clean clothes for you. We’ll already have a day in before you get there, so hurry.”

“I’ll be there in time for supper and some singing.”

* * * * *

That night, Cookie served up roasted turkey, stewed rabbits and fried squirrels.

“And won’t none of you find any bullet holes in any of the meat. That turkey didn’t have an eyeball on either side of its head, I want all of you to know.”

He shoved the men back who had crowded at the table.

“Hey, you all get back. No one’s passing through here ahead of Warren. Let him around the line—he’s first.”

The men pushed back and shouted at WC to come around, and hurry, before they all starved to death.

“I can wait my turn, sir.”

Pokey went back for the boy himself, dragging him by the arm to the front of the line.

WC took a plate and turned back to Pokey.

“I wanted to tell you that the day I hunted I was wishing Roy had sent you out with me.”

“You were? Well, thank you. I believe I could have helped.”

“Yes, sir, that’s what I thought. You see I got awful tired carrying all that meat by myself.”

Pokey shook his head and walked to the end of the line as everyone slapped him on the back.

The meal was not served to the usual grumbling and wariness. The men joked and talked. They had the good sense to avoid the killing and the rescue, but they made WC tell about the hunting. No one believed the part about "barking" the squirrel. Cookie backed him up.

"The danged thing didn't have a mark anywhere on it. Its neck was broke was all. I believe you knocked that bark off. I believe you did it. Don't believe you could do it again, though."

The whole week of work was less dreary. Every meal seemed a triumph. Roy tolerated prolonged lounging after lunch, an extra coffee, saying he did not know how they were doing it, but more timber was being sent out now than ever before.

At breakfast Saturday morning, Roy told the crew they were shutting down at noon, seeing how they had already put out more wood than any other week, and things were backing up at the mill. They would be paid for a full day—if there was no objection. The whooping and table thumping were the only signs of rebellion.

Later, when pay was handed out, WC was surprised to receive his full wage and a letter sealed in an envelope. He told Roy there was a mistake. Mr. O'Dell was to keep back part of his pay.

"That letter will explain things."

WC turned it over several times and put it in his back pocket.

"Aren't you going to read it? You might have a question."

"No, sir. Not now."

* * * * *

At Uncle Otis' he was met by aunts armed with hugs and kisses, hair-ruffling and cheek pinching. It was awful, but he liked it. Della squeezed him unusually hard.

"I have some big news."

"What?"

"Not now. Later. I have it all planned."

"Where's Tommy Irene?"

"She's inside—embarrassed to see you. You're the only other person to know what happened to her."

"How's she doing?"

"Blossoming, except she's worried about you."

"She doesn't have to worry about me."

"I know she don't, but she's just not sure."

Della was different to him—spoke eagerly. Her face had more color, and her entire body was taut with energy. She seemed poised to wing away.

"Be right back. Don't go away." She flew off to the house.

WC joined the few men grouped around a blazing fire beneath a caldron. It was piled to the brim with white slabs of hog fat. Everyone stood back from the heat, watching it render to a churning liquid. Uncle Otis was in charge of deep frying the fish.

"I reckon that'll cook a mess of Buffalo fish, don't you, WC?"

"It'll do fine, sir."

Della escorted a man to the fire. They walked arm in arm.

"WC, this is your Uncle Louis from Detroit."

He was a wide man with a guitar slung across his back. He stepped forward and shook WC's hand. His hair was thinning on top, but WC's mother, Aunt Clair, and Uncle Otis were definitely in his features. He wore a devilish expression on his face. WC liked him immediately.

"Last time I saw you, your ma brought you out in a bread pan."

"Louis, you big fat liar, it's not been that long."

He put his arm around her and squeezed until she squealed.

"Sis thinks the world of you."

"She's my ma, sir."

"She has reasons other than that," Otis declared.

Uncle Block joined them, nodded curtly at WC and took over the conversation. Della excused herself to rescue a toddler from the abundant affections of an over zealous cousin.

Bill Philip and Jimmy strolled up on either side of WC.

"Do you want to pitch washers?" Bill Philip nudged WC.

"Not right now, I don't."

"I already got the two holes dug. Let's play."

WC shook his head. "Don't feel like it."

He watched his mother. She was like a butterfly among the younger children. Landing a moment and being adored.

"Want to pitch quarters, then? Or you scared to do that?"

"Yeah, are you scared?" Jimmy slugged WC's shoulder.

WC pushed Jimmy away from him.

"You asked me what I wanted to do, and I told you."

Bill Philip shoved WC and crowded him, chest to chest.

Uncle Otis stepped in.

"How about you boys helping me cut up the fish?"

"Not me," Bill Philip retreated. "I don't like the smell of fish on my hands. Beside I was about to pitch washers with Jimmy and WC."

"I'll help, sir. I don't care anything about washers. What do you want me to do?"

"Run and get the knives from the kitchen. Louis and I will bring the tub of fish around."

Bill Philip caught WC's arm, and held his fist under his cousin's nose.

"I'll remember you made me look bad to Uncle Otis."

"Won't that be a test for your brain!" He went on to the house.

A group of knives lay in a shallow pan and Otis' wife, Ada, said they were the ones to be used for the fish.

"Do you know where Tommy Irene is?"

"Don't you come in here," her contrary voice shouted from behind the closed living room door.

"Why not? I've got a favor to ask."

"Get someone else."

"No. You're the only one."

There was a deliberating silence from the other side of the door.

"What is it?"

WC asked Aunt Ada if they could be alone. She smiled, dried her hands on a towel and went out the back screen door.

"It's a letter from my boss in Little Rock."

Without any hesitation she told him to slide it under the door.

"You can't tell anyone what it says, unless I say so."

"Ha. Who you going to get to read it if I don't?"

"I'll wait and have Mr. Bell do it next week end."

"You would, wouldn't you?"

"Yeah, but I'd rather you."

"I'll read it—I won't tell."

He pushed the letter under the door and heard the envelope being opened and stiff paper unfolded.

"Fancy paper, don't you know. Okay, here goes.

'The Lester O'Dell Banking—blah, blah, blah
Of Little—blah, blah

Master Warren Carl Thomas:'

" 'Master!' " Tommy jeered. " 'Master of what?' "

"Just read it, would you please."

"I'm going to. It says—

'I am sure you may have found your full wage a bit confusing, since you expected a portion to be withheld. The explanation is simple.

'The matter of Ullah Short and her children was presented to our dear Mrs. Shearcott, who has since enlisted charitable support from her faithful friends: The Cohn's Department Store, the Pfeifer's Department Store, Allsopp & Chapple Bookstore, Burrows Dry Goods, Hillis' Bakery, the G.N. Hart Drug Shop, and Blass' Grocery, Meats and Produce. These fine people have made a practice over the years of assisting those in need, and Mrs. Short's situation was readily addressed as soon as it was brought to their attention.

'She and each of her children have been medically examined. Thankfully, there are no serious offenses that salves will not cure. They will have continued yearly check ups and access to the physician whenever necessary. Smoked meats, canned goods, and other staples, enough to last through the winter will be delivered to them, along with clothing for each member of the family. Their needs will continue to be monitored and met.

'This experience has been our joy, and everyone has you to thank for it. When Alma told Mrs. Short how this endeavor was started, her lone remark was, 'He thought about us?' You have made us proud of you and proud of ourselves.

'Sincerely,

'Mr. Lester O'Dell'

"Did that make sense to you? I hardly made out what half them words meant. Who's Ullah Short?" She pushed the letter back under the door to him.

"Her husband was one of the killers. I'll tell you about it later. I've got to go help Uncle Otis."

They scaled and gutted the fish, cut the heads off and chunked each of them into hand-sized pieces. Otis liked them to sit in salt water at first to draw out any blood, and then he soaked them in milk. They would be breaded with salt, pepper, a little flour and corn meal and dropped in the grease to roil.

Uncle Block carried the pail of heads and offal away to be buried. Louis and Otis washed the knives and began slinging handfuls of water at each other. Then they were laughing and wrestling over possession of the dishpan, soaking their shirts.

Della called from the porch for them to behave.

"Is the fish ready?"

"All it wants is for you ladies to give the word," Otis answered.

"Well, not just yet. I have something to do first."

"Dancing or preaching?" Louis wanted to know.

"Well, today, I could do either one—or both for that matter. But I have an announcement, so bring everyone to the porch."

She bustled back inside the house. Family scattered throughout the yard were called to the porch to hear what Della had to say. WC shrugged at all the questions, feeling as much in the dark as anybody.

Della burst from the door leading Clair and Tommy Irene by the hand. The women smiled with the abundance of a secret, while the girl hid her eyes and fidgeted with a new dress. Tommy's usual pouting, peppery expression was obscured by a bashful attempt for poise. She bit her bottom lip and glanced out at the gathered family who had been offering compliments about how pretty she looked. Her freshly cut and curled hair shined vibrantly red. A grand bow held her bangs in place on the top of her head. She caressed self-consciously what fell around her ears.

WC recognized the velvet jacket she wore. It was the one he had gotten from Alma Shearcott. His mother had cut it down and remade it for Tommy Irene. It fit perfectly, tapering close to her waist before angling onto her hips.

She caught sight of WC. Though he was smiling her forehead knitted with annoyance. He winked. Her face relaxed and she took her teeth from her bottom lip. WC expected a smile, but her puckery look returned and she stuck out her tongue. The crowd laughed and he was relieved she was all right. Della kissed her on the cheek.

"There's something I want you all to know." Della put an arm around each of her companions and drew them close.

"The girls are here to hold me up—I need the help. Even though this is the happiest I've been in years, the news is hard to tell." She left Clair and Tommy Irene and moved to the edge of the porch.

"At first, when WC left home to work in that camp, I didn't care what happened to me. I was angry, empty as a pitcher with a crack in it. My life was good as over. But it wasn't; it didn't need to be. If my son could strike off on his own, then why should I fear what the rest of my life could be—ought to be. I stood face to face with a door. Who could know what was behind it—maybe worse than I was. Thank the Lord, there was courage to open it, and now I'm standing in sunlight."

She looked down at the steps, clasped her hands together and raised her eyes to meet WC's.

"Son, I've sold the house—sold out lock, stock, and barrel. There's not a thing back in Antioch to go home to. All our possessions have been loaded on Fisher's freight wagon and carried away."

The family stood motionless, mute, forsaking Della of any response.

Tommy Irene threw her arms around Della, hugging her tightly and knocking her bow cockeyed.

CHAPTER SEVENTEEN

THE HAT

Della hugged Tommy Irene wildly in return.

"You little darling, thank you."

Then questions began flowing.

Della retied the bow on Tommy Irene's head, while answering every one calmly.

"I'm moving to Little Rock. I have a room in a boarding house."

"No, Custer will not be coming with me."

"I did not sell my husband's house. I sold my house."

"I've not the foggiest idea what Custer's going to do. He's a grown man."

"I'll be working at a hotel—as a Floral Assistant."

"I did not have to be locked into that world, as if it were the only one."

"I don't know. The last I saw of him he was galloping off to his brother's house."

Louis told her she would have to start wearing shoes. City people did not care for naked feet.

"And I've already bought me new ones, haven't I Irene?"

"Yes, she did."

"She helped me pick them out. And a new dress. One for her, too."

Tommy spread the skirt and curtsied.

"She was with me the whole time—getting the job and the room. We rode the trolley from one end of town to the other. We even talked on a telephone."

Block called from the back of the small crowd.

"That's all pretty fancy, Della, but the long and short of it is you're leaving your man. Ain't ya? You're just up and calling it quits for Custer?"

"Yes I am, Block."

"Well, it don't seem right."

"I struggled with that very thing for a while, until I went back three years ago to where I first went wrong. I'm making up for it now, and I'm satisfied with my repentance for that mistake."

Block had to argue—it seemed he had something at stake.

"You disappoint me. Never thought you'd take to sin."

From the way most people turned and faced him, they did not feel he had much of a leg to stand on himself.

Della softened to Block's challenging tone.

"It is so"—she looked for the right words, "helpful, such a blessing, to be instructed in the matters of my transgressions. Where were you during my living with sin the past three years? How did that failing get past your careful examination of my life?"

WC spit into the dirt. Was the man stupid or so selfish he could not see? Just because you dig a hole does not mean you stand in it for the rest of your life and shut out the landscape. If his mother had not been doing so well by herself, he would have gone back himself and explained things a bit more forcefully, whatever the consequences.

Della folded her arms across her chest and cocked her head to one side. She was an adult image of Tommy Irene.

"Is there anything you care to add, Block Foster?"

WC thought she would have fought him right then and there— probably beaten him too, if Block's own wife had not saved him.

"If there's any sin, it's between her and the Lord," Clair told him. "So behave yourself, Daddy, and don't spoil Sister's happiness. She's determined herself and there's no turning back. Just you be careful yourself. You hear?"

She hugged Della and Tommy Irene again and invited everyone up to the porch. Aunt Ada led a small group of women and girls to embrace and congratulate Della. Other women were not as certain about her actions and were stand-offish. Two of the men shook their heads, and one of them made his way toward Block rubbing a hand against his whiskered face.

Otis stood on the steps.

"Folks, I suspect Sister has raised some eyebrows and will be the source of conversation for some time to come. But men, I don't believe we have to fear a general uprising of the womenfolk. At least, I hope, not until we eat. So Block, come and help me cook that fish."

Ada sent boys and girls to get saw horses and planks to make the table.

"Set it up in the shade. Then bring out the chairs and benches. Clair, would you check the collards and pull the cornbread out of the oven? Louis! Play that guitar! Let's have some music."

Louis strummed and everyone danced to their jobs, leaving Della and WC to themselves at the porch.

"Well, what do you think? Am I on my way to the fiery pit?"

She sat on the top step, resting her shoulder against the porch post. WC stood on the ground beside her, leaning against it.

"I not a preacher to answer such things, but it's good to see you so happy."

"Oh, I am, I truly am. And scared. But not so scared, though, as when Irene and I drove the mules into Little Rock. By the way, Mrs. Shearcott sends a 'Hello,' and she just fell in love with Irene."

She leaned around the post.

"And you were right about her Eddie—he's a piss ant."

"Ma!"

"Well, that's what he is." She pulled back.

"I know, but--"

She waved her choice of words away.

"Never mind me. I'm just crazy today."

"I don't know how you did it all."

"If you would have blinked an eye you would have missed us, the way we moved from one thing to another. Jocelyn O'Dell told me about the big hotel. Once they hired me, Irene and I found an affordable boarding house. We drove home the next day and went right away to see Alvin Dedge with my deed."

"How did you get him to pay for the house?"

She clapped her hands and shifted to the edge of the step.

"It was easier than I ever could have thought, because all he sees is a dumb ol' woman without shoes on. But I took him by surprise when I laid that deed on his porch railing and said I was giving him his only chance to buy the house. He wondered what I was talking about, and I told him I was determined to sell the property off, but was willing to give him the first chance to buy it. Oh, did he fuss and argue over that."

She deepened her voice.

" 'I'd be crazy to buy the house twice. You can't do that. We had us a deal.' "

"We kept the deal—I married Custer and you deeded me Sonny's land. But nothing was ever said about staying married. Especially to someone who takes a gun to my son.' "

She wrapped an arm around the post and leaned closer to WC.

"He shot at you that day the pigs were killed, didn't he? I'm asking you for truth, WC. Didn't he shoot at you?"

"I'm not sure, but he aimed at me a couple of times."

"I knew it! I'm well rid of him and plenty of other things as well."

"But go on—what happened next?"

"Anyway, Alvin tried bullying—threatening to sic lawyers on me. I just picked the deed up and said I'd sell it to him at a fair price, or I'd sell it to someone else for what I could get. And I would have. Told him I'd sell it for a quarter to the first person to come along, before I'd let it go back to him for less than what I wanted. And then he'd have no control over who lived there—he couldn't put his sharecropping family in it. I thought he was going to explode."

She imitated his voice again.

" 'It ain't right, Della! Where do you get off treating me this way after all I've done for you?' "

"He said I'd gotten the place for nothing, but I let him know the high price I'd paid. He <u>had</u> to buy it from me, and when I told him what I'd take, he almost choked to death."

She laughed and slapped her leg.

"I took less for it, but on top of that I got cash for our share of this year's crop. Irene and I had to walk out to the wagon with the deed and climb up into the seat before he would agree to that. We went right then to get the money and sign the deed over.

"Sold everything inside the house to Clyde Fisher and had him carry our personals into Little Rock. Poor ol' Custer stood around watching and scratching his head, wondering what in the world was going on."

She collapsed back on the porch with her arms spread wide.

"I am so relieved; so finished with things back there."

WC turned and lay on his side next to her, propping his cheek in his hand to look at her.

"It seems like you've been with the moon."

"And the stars and the sun and all the heavenly bodies."

She sat back up.

"Oh. I almost forgot."

She retrieved a package that had been sitting by the door.

"This is yours. Couldn't any of this have happened without you."

He held the box in his lap.

"What is it? I don't need anything."

"Open it up and see."

He cut the string with his jackknife, folded it back up and put it away. He lifted the lid from the box and set it beside him before looking inside.

It was a hat. A fedora like his daddy's.

"You like it?... WC?"

He finally nodded yes.

"Take it out. Try it on."

He touched the crown—ran his finger from front to back. He lifted it from the box, snapped the front brim down, creased the crown and dented the sides.

"Put it on. Let's see what it looks like."

He set it on his head and turned his face to her.

"Don't you like it?"

He nodded.

"Then don't be so serious—be a boy for a minute. A handsome hat like that needs a smile. Have a little fun. Hold on—let me get something."

She ran inside the house. The door had hardly closed before she had returned holding a hand mirror to his face.

"What do you think?"

He tipped the hat further to one side. Turned left and right to look at himself.

"I like it. I like it more than anything." He took the hat off.

"It needs one more thing."

He unbuttoned his bib pocket and reached inside, recovering the dandelion seed rolled in the dollar bill. He slipped it under the hat band and set it back on his head. He checked the mirror again and smiled slightly.

"You think I look like daddy?"

EPILOGUE

THE PATIO

A lifetime had passed. On a back porch concrete patio, I stood eating the remaining edge of an apricot fried pie, brushing the flaky debris from my clerical blouse, and watched him tussle with a squirming great, great grandchild. The baby's mother stood stroking the papery, smooth arms of her great grandmother.

"Granddad, don't let him wiggle you to death."

The old buzzard snorted.

"Don't think I've not had to hold on to slipperier things than this little squirt."

He almost made it to a hundred, but died three years short of it. Nearly the whole world came to his send off at the State Capitol. All his kids wanted me to have his hat, which I was proud to own, but just before the casket closed I placed it on his hands.

About the Author

Fred lives with his wife Joan near the beaches and dunes in Muskegon, Michigan. His three children and seven grandchildren are all within half a day's drive. He says, "Unless someone was completely delirious, it would have been impossible for them to have enjoyed themselves as much as I did in my thirty years in public education."